No nonsense Nikki Nolan is tired of being the bridesmaid and never the bride. Cupid has flat out lost his aim. Or maybe he confused Nikki's younger sister with her, since Caren's getting married — again!

But the real kicker? Nikki has two weeks to plan the wedding of the century . . . and in Hawaii, no less! So she coerces tourist agent and bad boy of Waikiki, Mark Wheaton, to co-plan the event. With access to an extensive network of contacts, Mark is the perfect person to help, even though she suspects he's more interested in luring her into his bed than picking out flower arrangements.

Will Cupid finally hit his mark, or will Nikki remain unhappily single?

Back to the Beach 1
Copyright © 2019 Kathy Kalmar
ISBN: 978-1-4874-2214-1
Cover art by Martine Jardin

Published by eXtasy Books Inc or
Devine Destinies, an imprint of eXtasy Books Inc

Look for us online at:
www.eXtasybooks.com or www.devinedestinies.com

BACK TO THE BEACH 1
BACK TO THE BREACH BOOK 1

BY

KATHY KALMAR

DEDICATION

Dedicated to Larry. Always, he's the best "alpha"/beta reader ever, reading every version, every time he's asked. His tact and patience are laudable.

MEMORANDUM

For Linda, whose counsel and presence I miss daily. Nikki Nolan could be her twin. This one's for you.

ACKNOWLEDGMENT

Carolyn Gilbreath, world's best beta reader, plotter, and close friend. Jay Austin, maker of dreams come true and EIC; Debbie Nygaard, editor; Martine Jardin artist; R.C. Matthews, beta reader; Doug Marple, webmeister; and the members of the Greater Detroit Romance Writers of America. A shout goes to my readers.

CHAPTER ONE: THE JITTERS

Nikki's heart raced. She jumped into her purple PT Cruiser and drove as quickly as she could to reach her nephew, Zach, his words still repeating in her mind. *Mom's freaking out!* That was all it took to get her there in a heartbeat. Zach answered the door when she arrived at her sister's house.

Emily, her niece, launched herself into a hug. "You're here!" She relinquished her hold when her mother, Caren, hugged her just as tight.

"You're my last hope." Caren rushed to Nikki's side and hugged her just as tight. Then she began to pace the floor, chewing her bottom lip and lacing her shaking fingers together.

"Whatever it is," Nikki warned, "don't make me say *No.*"

"Hear me out first."

Nikki glared at her.

Caren quickly added, "It's not that, I promise."

"It better not be. I'm not going to be your bridesmaid — again — and that's final. Seventeen times was enough!"

"Well, truth is, you only stood up for me once. The others weren't my doing. Is it my fault you have a lot of friends?"

Nikki ignored her sister's comment. "Besides, I thought Daisy is your Matron of Honor . . ."

"She is. Seriously, it's not that."

"Then what is it? What do you need?" she asked, now satisfied she would not be stuck with yet another ugly bridesmaid gown that would never see the light of day again.

"Be my wedding planner."

1

"What happened to the wedding planner you already have?"

"I fired her," Caren replied with a sigh, her green eyes luminous with about-to-be shed tears.

"Why on earth would you do that?" Nikki shrieked.

"For starters, no venue, no flowers, no cake, no priest, and no food. Need I go on?"

"Yes!"

"If that's not enough, she called me an absent-minded Bridezilla."

"The absent-minded part is true"—she mumbled under her breath, then added louder—"but the wedding is only two weeks away."

Caren let out a whoosh of air. Her red waves moved as she nodded. "I knew you'd get it."

Nikki shook her head. "And you defend your dissertation Thursday morning!"

"Yes."

"You know I'm a therapist—a reality therapist, I might add—not a magician." She would have laughed if Caren was not so upset.

Moving her arms around randomly, Caren looked rattled to her core, shooting off sparks of anxiety and biting her lips. She reached for her lip balm and smoothed it on her tortured lips—always a sign her sister was worried.

Nikki stayed calm while Caren emoted, then she took charge. Physically, the sisters were as opposite as their polar personalities. Caren was petite, not short, as she'd be the first to point out—not that she would ever call Caren short. Nikki was statuesque by comparison, with generous curves. While Caren had long waves of red hair, her own hair was copper-colored, fine and straight, cut in a bob with bangs.

But she wasn't thinking about similarities, or differences for that matter. Heaven help her, she was thinking like a wedding planner!

"You're still sold on a destination wedding, right?" At Caren's nod, she pressed on. "Travel arrangements are made?" Again, Caren nodded. "Chance's doing, I presume?"

Caren just grinned and shrugged.

Chance Matthews was soon to be Nikki's new brother-in-law. Caren and Chance had met on a tour to Hawaii. Now they were about to be married.

"Good, that's done. Next, I need to talk to whatshisname at the whatchamacallit?"

"Who?" Caren looked at her with a blank expression.

"What's that guy's name at the tour company you went through for your first trip? You're using them, right?"

"Sorta."

"What's that mean? Either you are or you aren't."

With a telling grin, Caren admitted, "Truth be told, the wedding planner was handling all that. I'm not sure about whether she made reservations."

"All righty then, for sure I need his name and number. Pronto."

Caren complied. "His name is Mark Wheaton at World Travel and Tour."

"He's the handsome hunk you dated briefly, right? The George Clooney clone?"

"Yes, *Miracle Mark*, you called him."

"At that time, it took a miracle to get you to smile again."

"What's he got to do with this?"

"Everything, my dear little sister, everything. Now, you leave *Mission Impossible* to me and go . . . go defend something," she finished as she programmed the phone number into her contact list.

Obviously, Caren didn't need to be told twice. She went back to her computer to prepare to defend her dissertation and earn her doctorate. The whole time she'd worked on her

thesis, her mantra had been *Go big, or go home.*
Guess she ought to know.

Caren had absolutely no time for anything but her preparation. Currently, she was an assistant professor of English at the University of Michigan. She either earned her doctorate and kept her job, or she had neither. She couldn't spare a moment to deal with botched wedding plans, and Nikki was happy to step in to help.

Nikki's mind raced as she processed the fact that she had taken on planning a wedding in two short weeks. Then she shrugged. *How hard could this wedding business be? Seriously.*

She called World Travel and Tour and set an appointment for the next morning with Mark Wheaton. Bidding her family goodbye, she left for her condo.

As she prepared for the morning, she made notes while deciding to wear her sleeveless coral sheath for the meeting. It did wonders for her. *What can it hurt to look my best? You never know . . . Didn't I say something like this to Caren a few months ago? She might meet someone? I could, too. Mark's a hunk. Anything could develop.* Despite the possibilities, she was sure it would be a headache, not a romance. Still, a girl could hope.

She arrived at World Travel and Tour bright and early ready to meet with Mark Wheaton.

"Good morning. May I get you some coffee, juice, water?" Jane Addison, the office manager, greeted.

"Hello. No. I'm fine. I'm here to see Mark Wheaton for our appointment."

A slight furrow creased Jane's smooth forehead indicating some chagrin as she said under her breath, "I hope you have a smartphone or an e-reader." Speaking louder she clarified, "Mr. Wheaton hasn't arrived yet. Let's make you comfortable and I'll get that coffee. It's a gourmet blend, and it's delicious. Straight from Kona."

Nikki looked at her watch. "I have work to do. The

appointment was for nine sharp."

Jane nodded. "I know, and I'm sure something has kept him. Traffic can be a bear this time of day, especially with all the road construction. Mark is very good at what he does. He pulls off miracles."

Nikki shifted her weight, one hand on her hip, her foot tapping in irritation and pent-up frustration. "He'd better, I need one. But I navigated that traffic as well as you, and we are here. On time."

Jane handed her the Kona coffee and wisely kept quiet. Mark's reputation preceded him — he was known to party and play the field.

Nikki fumed as she waited, drumming her fingers on the end table holding out-of-date, well-worn magazines. *The least he could do was provide something current to read! Cheez.* She picked up an old copy of *Faces.* After reading it, she still didn't recognize any of those faces. *The only face I want to see is Mark's.*

Caren had told her about her few dates with Mark. Probably being a pretty boy — no, make that a playboy — most likely made him feel entitled to be late. With women hanging all over him, it was probably his standard operating procedure. *Well, I'm not one of those women!*

She resented the wait. *He should make an effort to be here on time.* No doubt he couldn't be bothered with a little thing like a business appointment.

A full thirty minutes later, Nikki rose to leave the office to add money to the parking meter when the door burst open and she collided with the hardest chest she had ever run into — literally. The force knocked her clutch-purse out of her hand. They both went down to retrieve it at the same time and knocked heads.

His hand reached out to steady her.

Something electric surged through her. *Did he feel it too?*

"Fancy running into you, like this," Mark quipped helping her to her feet and retrieving her purse. "Are you ok?"

"Mark Wheaton, I presume," Nikki ground out.

"The one and only," he replied with an appreciative glint in his eye.

Smooth operator. Nikki looked up into warm chocolate eyes. Her retort died on her lips when she felt a jolt—again—from his touch as she accepted her purse. Swallowing hard, she said, "We, we have an appointment."

"More like a date with destiny."

She attempted to straighten herself when he smiled.

Nikki cleared her throat to recover her self-control. "Whatever. We had an appointment that started thirty-five minutes ago. I'm Nikki Nolan, Caren Michelson's sister."

Grinning sheepishly, looking like a schoolboy, Mark ushered her into his well-appointed office. She could feel his gaze traveling her figure. Despite herself, she was attracted to him and didn't like it one little bit. Her normal composure was shot and she worked to retrieve it. She was not amused, nor was she flattered by his frank appraisal. He gestured to a seat and she took it.

"What can I do to help you?" Mark, too, appeared to struggle from his too-close-for-comfort contact with her body.

She was secretly pleased he seemed rattled. However, she needed his help, and his cooperation was necessary if she had any chance at all to get Caren's wedding launched. "Do you remember Chance Matthews and Caren Michelson and the trip they booked with you last spring?" Nikki began.

"How can I ever forget that public relations promo?" Mark groused. "What about them? And more importantly, what does that have to do with me?"

"Everything, and more. This is your golden opportunity to turn that fiasco around and get some positive press too."

His eyebrows rose. "How's that? I've already taken care of them. Evacuations. Refunds. Vouchers for another trip. All of it was an act of God. Beyond my control. What more can I do?"

With practiced calm, she looked him straight in the eyes. "Sponsor their wedding."

"What?" he sputtered. "Why?"

"Because the volcano eruption can be flipped and capitalized on. You can build on that act of God with a *do-over* that can become your biggest PR coup yet. Chance and Caren met on your tour and fell in love on that trip. There's a myriad of PR potential with that alone, and yet I can see you've done nothing with it."

He crossed his arms protectively across his chest, and the movement outlined his broad shoulders. "How do you know that?"

She gestured to the brochures next to her. "I had plenty of time to read through your advertisements, and nada, not one hint of their story or them. Moreover, they fell in love with World Travel and Tour Company, too. There could be even more to promote, since they are using your company for their honeymoon."

Checking his computer, Mark asked, "They're honeymooning with us?"

"As of now, yes."

He shook his head, confused. "I don't see their reservation, accommodations, itinerary, nothing."

"That's why I'm here. Their wedding planner failed to, well, to plan their wedding. Obviously, she didn't make the reservations."

He scrubbed a hand across his lightly stubbled chin.

Nikki recognized the signs—hangovers were a bitch.

"Frankly, I still don't see what this has to do with me."

"I'm getting to that. When you sponsor their wedding, you'll have a PR mecca to exploit. You'll have a ton of happy tourists raving about you and your loyalty to them. Your business should skyrocket."

7

Understanding crossed his tanned features. "Capisce. I'm beginning to get the picture," he said slowly.

"Simply use your list server, and you can call in those vouchers." Nikki ticked her points off on her fingertips. "Invite those clients back to Kauai for Chance and Caren's wedding. Those folks are already vested in Caren and Chance, since their story was the talk of the tour. Then there's the other couple who met and married on the tour, too. With proper massaging, you'll be the hero and World Travel and Tour will be *the* premium and caring company to use."

Mark nodded. "I forgot about Daisy and Gus Weaves . . . You're right. We have not handled the potential PR there."

"It's built-in advertising. Everyone loves weddings. It'll save you a bundle and generate lots of rave reviews."

Mark's brow furrowed. "There's a lot of potential there, all right."

"Precisely! I'm not asking you to pay for the festivities, just to *plan* them. Use your connections, contacts, ties. Chance and Caren will pay, no problem with that."

Mark no longer looked bothered or concerned with that. Apparently, *he* was in planning mode and obviously excited. "We have exclusive rights to the Coconut Plaza Hotel. There's a chapel and everything right on site."

"A luau and flowers are easy enough to get. It is a tropical island. Flowers are all over the place."

"Look, uh, Nicole, I need to think about this more. Let's talk it over. Say dinner tonight?"

"We don't have the time. With a wedding to plan. It's coming up fast," she said. "And it's Nikki. Call me Nikki."

"Huh?"

"My name is Nikki. I don't use Nicole. Get it straight."

"Uh, oh, right. Most people have a year to plan their wedding." He chuckled. "I'd say we have plenty of time."

"No, we don't. The wedding is two weeks from Tuesday."

Chapter Two: In Shock

"But . . . but Tuesday! What the heck!" Mark sputtered. "There are all sorts of things to do. Why there's, uh, food. I don't know, uh, flowers . . . there's food and flowers." He finished in triumph.

Nikki laughed. "Careful there, you sound like a wedding planner."

He grimaced. "I do, don't I?"

"Exactly," Nikki agreed. "Let's get to work."

He and Nikki planned for several hours to create the fastest *wedding of the century* — as they began to call it. With a groan, Mark ran his hand across his stomach when it grumbled, then he suddenly sprang to his feet. "Come on," he said grabbing Nikki by the hand. He was famished now that his hangover was abating.

He all but lifted Nikki from her seat — and into his arms — in his rush to get her going. He paused for a moment when the current charged between them again. He felt the tingles shoot straight through him and was confused by his body's immediate reaction. It was hot like fire and twice as deadly.

What am I doing? I'm agreeing to this nonsense? His head was reeling just from his brief contact with her. He couldn't be doing this. *I'm thinking with the wrong head.* He felt overwhelmed, enraptured by her confidence, her no-nonsense attitude . . . her body. He wasn't sure he had felt like this before — ever.

"We have no time to waste," he said pulling her in his wake as they went through the office door. He called over his shoulder to Jane as they left. "I'll be at the Mauna Loa. Call ahead

9

and get my usual table."

Reeling at the shock of his attraction to her touch, he wondered if he'd met his match.

"Lagoon Room, no problem," Jane confirmed.

He turned back to Nikki and looked her straight in the eyes. "You felt that. I know you did."

"I bet you say that to all the girls. Is this where I blush, smile, and bat my eyes like so?" she asked batting her eyes in mock innocence.

"No, this is where *I* blush," he admitted. "Unfortunately, and maybe for the first time, that was no line. It was the simple truth. I felt that, and so did you."

"Uh-huh, sure," she huffed. "So what?"

"So?" he retorted. "Adults usually act on that."

"Not this one," she was quick to say.

Grabbing his suit jacket and hooking it over his shoulder, he led her out to the parking structure. "I'll drive."

She sent him a look that could toast bread but surprisingly didn't protest.

As Mark opened the car door, he wondered if she'd find it fun to slide into the black leather seat of his classic red Corvette with a — if he did say so himself — handsome dude in attendance. It didn't take long to reach his destination as he drove through the streets with skill and practiced ease.

He pulled up to valet parking for the Polynesian-themed restaurant, the Mauna Loa. As they entered through the huge dark-stained intricately carved set of double wooden doors, they were met by the hostess, who lifted delicate shell leis from the stand. Walking over to Nikki, Mark stopped the hostess, taking a lei from her hand.

"Here, let me." He draped the strand over Nikki's head and carefully kissed her, first on one cheek, then the other. "It's an ancient Hawaiian tradition," he said with a wink to Nikki. The hostess nodded.

Nikki resisted the urge to touch her cheek where he'd kissed it. She was sure her skin was seared. *Good thing I don't wear glasses. They'd be steamed up from the rising heat.* Her skin felt scorched from the touch of his lips. When she looked down to her hands, she almost expected to see blisters where they'd touched earlier. *Even contacts would have melted from this heat.*

The young girl led them into the Lagoon Room. Clearly, she knew Mark's preferences. Her familiarity and flirting gave credence to that.

"Your usual table?" she asked.

Nikki's brow quirked. "Do you come here often, then, Mark?"

"I do. Two Mai Tais?"

"I don't recall asking for one," Nikki huffed.

"I'm sorry. Force of habit."

"Do you usually order drinks for all the women you bring here?"

"I suppose I do."

"And do those women mind that you take it on yourself to decide what they want to drink?" Nikki probed her lips, set in a firm line.

"No one ever said they didn't like it. I thought women want men to be men."

"I don't know about other women, but this one likes to make her own choices."

Nikki smiled to herself as Mark squirmed uncomfortably, then he deftly changed the subject.

"I like this restaurant. I come here as often as I can. I like the food and ambiance. It's authentic. See that outrigger over there?" He gestured. "It's real."

"The décor is flawless," Nikki said. "I'm amazed they actually put in water for the lagoon."

"It's modeled after a place on Oahu. They went through a lot with customs to bring the vegetation over. The place is climate controlled to keep things growing. I do eighty percent of *W T and T* business in the Hawaiian Islands. I guess I miss Hawaii when I'm in Michigan. This is about as close to it as I can get unless I go to Florida."

"W T and T?"

"Sorry. Shop talk. It means World Travel and Tour Company Incorporated."

"I can see why you shorten it." She laughed and sipped her drink. "I'm glad I didn't send this back."

Surprise covered his face. "You'd have sent it back? Because I ordered it instead of you?"

"Damn straight."

"Why didn't you?"

She giggled and sipped. "I made my point." Then smiling she added, "I wanted to taste it, after all."

"Wait till you taste the real thing when there's sand or surf between your toes. There's nothing like it on earth."

"It's a strong drink for lunch isn't it?"

"What are you, an AA counselor?" he groused.

Is he a tad defensive? Does he have problems with alcohol? "Something like that. I'm a therapist with special certification for substance abuse. Too much of my work deals with the misuse of alcohol."

"But you're not at work now, and you are drinking it."

"I *was* drinking it," she corrected. "I've seen the damage alcohol does, and I generally don't take its use lightly. However, that's neither here nor there. We really need to discuss the wedding."

"Party pooper," he teased. "I was thinking I can use the shaman on the island to perform the ceremony, if you want a Hawaiian flavor."

"I'm sure they do. Using the chapel on the Coconut Plaza Hotel grounds will work, too. I got quite a lot of feedback after my sister's trip. Plus I've seen every photo known to man of the grounds. The venue's perfect."

"Were you kidding about a luau?"

"No, I think with so little lead time, it would be just the thing, don't you? Will a cake be a problem?"

"Only if we ask for one shaped like a volcano," he joked.

Nikki knew Kilauea had erupted on *W T and T's* last spring trip. It caused all sorts of commotion, necessitating cutting the trip short for some while others were given accommodations on other islands to continue their vacation.

"Wait! Perfect. That's it! A lava cake. After their experiences with a volcanic eruption last time they were in Hawaii, it'll add a touch of humor. My sister will love it."

"I like it."

She and Mark continued planning as their Mahi Mahi arrived. Changing the subject, he asked, "Do you do wedding planning on the side or what?"

She chuckled. "Hardly. This is an act of love and necessity. My baby sister is beside herself."

"Over the wedding?"

"No. She is completing her doctoral degree as we speak. If she fails to defend it, she loses money, time, her career, and her current job. When I heard her wedding planner had been fired, I did what any good sister would do. I stepped in."

"Sounds like you do that a lot."

"Do what a lot?" His comment had got her dander up.

"Relax. I meant it as a statement, not a criticism. I sense you step up to the plate as needed."

"I would do anything for my sister. She'd do it for me in a heartbeat."

"I get it, but don't you get enough of that at work?"

"It's not as much as it sounds. Caren has had it tough. Getting her education, getting a divorce, raising two children, completing her doctorate. She has her hands full right now.

It's temporary. This too shall pass."

"But who looks out for you?"

"I do." She smiled ruefully. "I take care of myself. Besides, right now, I have you." She realized what she'd said, and her cheeks heated. "To help with this wedding, I mean."

"Hmm. I see. I'm not just talking about this momentary crisis with the wedding. I wonder about the rest of the time? What about when you're tired from all the baggage people bring you, what happens with you then?"

"There is no significant other to hold my hand," she said. "I get by with my cat, Candy . . ." She glared at him when he smiled. "What?"

"A candy cat?" He chuckled. "A cat lady, then?"

She bristled. "Hey, watch it. I am not the proverbial *Cat Lady*. I don't have thirty cats, and I do have friends and family. I have a life." She didn't really take offense. "My cat is sweet, hence her name, thank you very much." Turning the tables, she asked, "What about you? No ring? Late nights? Flings? How do you cope? Do you, perhaps . . . par-tay?"

"Touché," he said, backing down.

By the end of the lunch, Nikki agreed to meet with Mark the next day after she finished work. She gave him a lot of ideas to work with, and there were contacts that only he could make. Mark seemed to be wavering, perhaps giving into his better self. As though he *should* help with the planning, for her, for her family.

He was one of the few people who truly could help, with very little effort on *W T and T's* part. He had the staff to make the calls, set the details in motion. She noticed the small, decisive nod he made, and she knew he was on board. He'd have to be a real hard-ass not to help.

Arriving back at the office, they made their goodbyes, each leaving to complete their separate tasks. Nikki retrieved her cruiser and drove to her office for her four o'clock appointment.

Owning her own practice had its perks. She liked helping people navigate the currents of life, and she loved setting her own hours. If memory served, she was meeting with Deidre Brewers, who was wrestling her demons with alcohol.

How serious a problem does Mark have? She was too experienced and too good at her job not to notice the signs—red eyes, day old stubble, and a drink with lunch. She had had one, too, but she did not have a problem. *Does Mark?*

CHAPTER THREE: WEDDING PLANNERS

Thinking about Mark and drinking in the same sentence distressed Nikki. A drinking problem was a deal breaker for her. Not that there was any *deal* to break, she reminded herself.

Nikki needed to talk to Caren about a Master of Ceremonies and music. She knew they'd want an authentic ceremony, so she wasn't worried about the food, flowers, or lava cake, but she wanted feedback on a few details. Like her dress, for one. Nikki wondered if Caren had time to even give that a thought. All she had on her mind lately was keeping her job. A quick call to Caren before Deidre arrived could get some of these things resolved.

"Hey," she began once she got Caren on the line. "Good news. Mark will handle most of the details. Speaking of details, I have a few questions for you."

"Wahoo!" Caren responded. "What do you need?"

"What about a Master of Ceremony and music for the reception?"

"My head is full of statistics and power points for my defense. Can't you call Chance or Mark?" she pleaded. "Wait . . . there was a guy in a lounge in Oahu. We really liked him. Ask Mark about getting Kekoa for an MC. And before you ask, I actually *did* take care of my gown myself. I'm using Gram's. I had the bishop sleeves removed and had it cut to tea length. It reminds me of the falls at the Seven Pools in Hana. I had it altered like one of those hi-low gowns—higher in front, longer in back. It's not too long, though, so it won't get wet during the ocean photo shots. It's perfect. I was thinking of a wreath of gardenias for my hair, and I want to carry a gardenia and daisies as a bouquet."

"Good to know at least some decisions are made," Nikki said checking off her list and making a note for gardenias. "I'll get Mark to order gardenias and I suppose Vanda orchids. Emily's the flower girl, right? Will a single gardenia be big enough for a bouquet?" Realizing Caren was preoccupied, she decided to figure it out and Caren would love it no matter what she selected. She made a note to secure a photographer.

Before she hung up, Caren confirmed, "Yes, Emily's doubling as a junior bridesmaid, too. Gotta go."

Her call completed, Nikki left Caren to work and went to begin her own for the day.

Looking around her office, Nikki was glad she'd taken time to create a welcoming décor. It was a small den with a loveseat, plenty of comfy cushions, and natural lighting.

She had a small antique secretary she used as a desk for billing while she sat in a spindle rocking chair. There was another rocker cattycorner to hers for those who needed movement. Her next appointment occupied it now.

Deidre had been seeing Nikki for well over a year. She was an alcoholic — soon to be a recovering one, Nikki hoped. Deride always set the rocking chair moving at quite a clip.

"I don't have a problem," Deidre said. "I don't miss work. I get things done. I just like to drink."

"Um-hmm," Nikki said encouraging her to continue.

"I don't do benders, or binges for that matter," she repeated. "I don't mess up at work either. I don't drink during the day —"

"What about lunch? Bloody Mary breakfasts?" Nikki reminded.

"I don't think that counts," Deidre countered. "There's

food to absorb it. It's not a problem."

"Then why are you here?" Nikki asked.

"I'm here because my marriage ended, and my kids are acting up. I just don't see the connection between my relaxing with drinks and a problem."

"That's precisely my point," Nikki insisted. "You don't see your very attitude is part of the problem. It's classic denial."

"Ouch! What happened to your bedside manner?" Deidre grumbled.

"I don't do gentle," Nikki said. "I do real. Reality can be a bitch. Alcohol will kill you and maybe someone else. Now we can play around here, or we can begin that Twelve Step program we've been talking about for the past four months."

Nikki's patience for alcohol abuse was wearing thin. She was seriously contemplating eliminating the substance abuse sector of her practice. It was much too destructive a disease. Maybe she needed a vacation.

She hoped against hope Mark didn't have a problem—not that it mattered to her one way or another. She fought to drive thoughts of her lunch with Mark out of her mind and turned her focus back to Deidre before it was too late for her help.

"I noticed that you have not talked about your kids moving in with their dad," Nikki continued. "Do you call that a problem? Your marriage is gone, now your kids."

Deidre increased the pace of her rocking.

Nikki noted she was hitting on very sensitive ground.

The session ended, a short time later, without the progress Nikki hoped to see. Turning off her office lights, she headed for home and her cat. *Tomorrow's another day. Hmm, I'll be seeing Mark again after work tomorrow. I better check my notes so I'll be ready.*

She fixed herself a cheese and mushroom omelet as she fed her cat. Curling up on the couch, she and Candy Cat fell asleep before *New Jersey Housewives* ended.

The next morning passed quickly, and Nikki found herself thinking of the buff brown-haired hunk more than once. He didn't need to express concern about her and her life for her to see genuine interest in those brown eyes of his. Their lunch had covered a wide range of topics, and despite herself, Nikki did enjoy his company. To his credit, he did flirt—true enough—but he had not overtly hit on her per se. Nikki felt she had made it clear she was not going to be part of his harem. She was equally clear about her likes and dislikes. Still, he was easy on the eyes and easy to talk to. *He does spice things up.*

Nikki freshened her makeup, straightened her silk blouse and capris, and adjusted the thin green belt at her waist. The biking she was doing before and after work did seem to be firming her curvy body after all.

Nikki wanted to lose weight, even though her full figure flattered her frame. She liked to think of herself as lush—well, maybe plush was more like it—but it was important to her to be as fit as possible.

After her last client of the day, she locked the door behind her as she left to keep her appointment with Mark. Fortunately, the rush hour traffic was not yet in full swing. She found a parking spot easily and entered *W T and T.*

Hearing her voice, Mark went to the outer office when Nikki entered. If it was possible, she looked even better than his mind had painted her. True, he had her dressed in less— much less—but what met his eye was mighty fine. "Come on, The day's over. I'm starved."

"But we have a meeting . . ." Nikki protested. "The wedding planning . . ."

"Will get done, I promise," he finished. "But how much can we accomplish when we need to eat?" Turning her by her shoulders, he firmly nudged her toward and out the door.

Mark made it clear he was not about to be deterred and was pleased she went along with him.

"What'll it be?" he asked, opening the car door and helping her slide into the deep bucket seat, "Chinese? Italian? Steak? Seafood?" Getting no response, he grinned. "Cat got your tongue? See what happens when I include you in the decision? Help me out here."

She looked chagrined but finally smiled. "Seriously, we have to stop meeting like this. I'm going to gain weight!"

He gave her a coy smile, and she seemed to respond to his charm.

She tilted her head, thinking for a moment. "Hmm . . . . French!"

At that, they both laughed outright.

He found her downright refreshing, not like his usual type. "Sacré Bleu!" He slapped the steering wheel emphatically.

"I wouldn't go that far," she retorted.

"No, that's the perfect restaurant! I know the maître d'."

"But of course," she said keeping their French-toned banter going. "Isn't it impossible to get in there without a reservation?"

"Just so happens I do a great deal of business there. I have a standing reservation I can call in. Never fear. You said French, and that's what the lady will get."

Nikki looked as if she was fighting not to be both excited and impressed. The restaurant's reputation was superlative. She sank back in her seat as Mark deftly maneuvered their way through the rush hour traffic. They arrived soon after and pulled into the valet parking. They were greeted warmly when they entered.

"*Mon ami*," the willowy blonde hostess greeted, kissing him European style on both cheeks.

"Monique," he responded taking her hand, bowing as he kissed it. "You are looking ravishing. So good to see you again." Surprising himself, he immediately ignored Monique and glanced back at Nikki. *She's hot!*

The upscale dining room was furnished with French Provençale furniture and looked really quite elegant. He saw her eyes light up.

"Wine?" Monique queried, handing Mark the wine list.

He glanced at Nikki for her guidance. At her slight nod, he proceeded, laughing lightly as he carried the French accent further. "Surely. May I suggest a Pinot Grigio, or would you prefer a Merlot? Whatever your heart desires, mademoiselle."

Nikki agreed to a Merlot.

Mark was trying not to go all manly on her. He wasn't going to make choices for her, and he planned to be considerate, not showy. He was behaving less and less the macho man he knew himself to be. At first he had taken her wishes for granted instead of asking her preferences assuming he knew best. Now, he knew better.

Then he reconsidered and recalled Monique's greeting. To his credit, he knew he wasn't watching Monique's progress across the room as she led another couple to a table. Normally, he couldn't keep his eyes off a retreating woman's ass.

Over their wine, Nikki quickly got to the matter at hand, her sister's wedding. She tapped her tablet and dove right in. "Caren said Kekoa might make a good Masters of Ceremony. What do you think?"

"Excellent choice. He's familiar with their story, works for us. We can make that happen easily enough."

"Oh, and we need a wreath of gardenias, Vanda orchids, daisies, and leis for the bride and groom . . ."

" . . . and leis for the guests," Mark added making notes on his tablet. "Anything else?" He looked up just as their à la carte entrées arrived.

"Yes, music for the ceremony. When we aren't using authentic Hawaiian drums, that is." She winked with a saucy smile.

"Torchlight ceremony, I trust?" he asked as he speared the perfectly prepared asparagus.

"Um-hmm . . . oh this is to die for!" she nodded, then took another bite of the flavorful food.

As they cleansed their palette between servings with sorbet, he decided to push his luck. "Can you get away and head over to the isles ahead of the wedding? There are details you have to experience before we can proceed."

She swallowed fast. "What? Get away? Now? What details?"

"TJ and the Sharks, for one."

"The who and what?"

Mark chuckled. "TJ and the Sharks. They're an island group that is up and coming, but you really have to hear them and decide for yourself whether they're right for you. So how 'bout it? You game for an earlier flight over to Oahu?"

"Oahu? I thought the wedding venue is Kauai."

"It is, but *The Hat Check Lounge* is on Oahu."

"A wedding planner has to do what a wedding planner has to do," Nikki huffed. "Being in the business, I trust your office will handle all the arrangements?"

"Will do. I think we'll stay at the Moana if" — he cocked an eye in her direction — "you have no objections?"

"None whatsoever." She grinned. "Waikiki beach?"

"Yes. It is the very first hotel built on the island. I think you'll enjoy it. It's a short walk to *The Hat Check Lounge* where TJ and the Sharks play."

Before the evening ended, Nikki agreed to leave for Oahu on Saturday. He knew she wasn't planning to frolic in the tropics, but it'd be criminal not to show her around.

Who was he kidding? He was more than ready for some fun after the heavy demands of his job. He was sure she'd earned some time off, some frivolity, too. Her life was no barrel of laughs.

"You're quiet," Mark said as they drove back to his office so she could get her car.

"Just thinking, always thinking."

"About?"

"Fun in the sun."

"My kind of girl."

She shook her head. "I don't think so."

"No? Why?"

She smirked. "You strike me as a bit of a player."

"Ouch." He grimaced. "You just softened that didn't you?"

With no malice in her tone, she said, "I think you can be a bit of a cad."

Aggravated, Mark stepped on the accelerator. "You think?"

"I could be wrong, but I don't think so."

"Then I think I'm insulted," he said dropping her off at her car.

He waited for her to get safely behind the wheel of her vehicle, then he smashed his accelerator. His tires screeched as he sped away laying rubber on the road.

Oops. Too direct, but what the heck. Ah tells it as ah sees it.

Nikki drove over to Caren's to bring her up to date. She didn't get the chance, because Daisy and Gus Weaves, their recently *adopted parents,* pulled up into the drive just as Nikki arrived. Getting out of the car, Daisy wrapped her in a warm hug. Gus did the same.

Daisy and Gus and Caren's family had stayed closely in touch since their shared trip with *W T and T* to Hawaii where they all met. Gus and Daisy were on the sunny side of seventy and had become *grandparents* to Caren's kids and as close as parents to Caren, Chance, and Nikki. Gus was giving Caren away at the wedding.

Nikki followed the couple into the house and greeted the children amid their happy cries — Gus was carrying a pizza.

"Whoopee, Pizza!" Emily squealed as she hugged them. "What kind?"

Gus winked. "Pineapple! In honor of the occasion."

"You two are a gift from God, no two ways about it," Caren cried, scarfing a piece down as quickly as possible. "Your room is ready. Make yourselves at home."

"You go on now, Caren," Daisy counseled. "By the looks of it, you have a lot on your mind."

Quick tears welled and fell from Caren's eyes. "I'm so grateful you're here. I defend tomorrow, and I cry at the drop of a hat. I don't know what's wrong with me!"

"Just a little thing like a wedding, and a defense. You go on now. Go work. We'll take care of everything," Gus remarked.

"How's Caren doing?" Daisy asked Nikki once things settled down and Caren returned to her home office.

"You heard she fired the wedding planner?" Nikki asked.

Daisy looked concerned. "Yes, and you and Mark are taking the wedding over, correct?"

Nikki frowned slightly. "That's right. On Saturday, Mark and I are leaving for Oahu to do some planning that has to be done face-to-face."

"You and Mark?" Daisy smiled as if she knew something Nikki didn't.

Noticing, Nikki groused, "It's not like that. We're co-wedding planners, that's all, and there are details we need to be on site for."

"Like what, dear?"

"Like . . . This is not a romance in the making, I mean."

"If you say so, dear."

"He's mad at me anyway."

"Mad?"

"I called him a playboy."

Daisy's lips quivered as if she was repressing a smile. "A playboy?"

She grimaced. "Actually, I called him a cad."

"I see. These things have a way of working themselves out. Now, tell me about Caren and the plans."

Nikki did. She, too, had noticed Caren was in tears more often than not. She and everyone else—especially Chance— would be glad when it was over.

She knew Chance was in an awkward spot, as he was the new Dean of the department and would be there for Caren's defense. The pressure was on them both. Nikki explained how Caren's committee had played games and had delayed her review over and over again, dragging it ever closer to her wedding day.

The facts were that committees did raise the stakes as the doctoral wheels turned. The entire procedure was designed to increase the pressure on Caren to see if she could buck up and perform under fire, but knowing the score didn't seem to help Caren one little bit. As the night drew to a close, Nikki drove home thinking of what the next days would bring, grateful that Gus and Daisy were there to help.

The next morning, Caren wore a fitted black dress with a rose print scarf tied professionally around her throat. She had her laptop and thumb drive at the ready and was as prepared as she could be. Every night for the last month had been spent practicing her presentation. She reviewed it as she fell asleep, presenting it differently each time so it would flow and not come off as scripted or rehearsed. She had so many versions prepared that she hoped it would come off smoothly.

Kissing everyone goodbye, Caren headed for the door. Gus and Daisy were on hand in case the children needed them.

Just as she grabbed the doorknob, Emily ran up to her.

"Mommy! Mommy! Are you gonna give shots after today?"

Zach smacked his forehead. "She's not that kind of doctor, dork."

"Call her *Emily*, not *dork*." Caren's correction was automatic. "No shots, Sweet Pea."

"Can I call you Dr. Mommy?" Emily asked.

Caren chuckled. "Now, that's a *yes!*"

"So long, Doc-to-be," Zach said.

Gus gave her a thumbs-up sign. "Break a leg."

"No need for tears. Not even happy ones," Daisy teased.

Caren left for the campus. The university community had been notified she was defending. Her colleagues, committee members, and Chance, the Dean of her department, were there. Quick tears sprang to her eyes when Nikki walked into the conference room in support of her.

Her chairperson, noticing Caren choke up, mouthed *What's wrong?* Caren smiled, gave him a thumbs-up, and blinked the tears away, then took a deep breath, and began.

Nikki had seen her sister perform in a variety of professional capacities in the past, but she had never seen this Caren before. She was clear, concise, precise, polished, and her eyes were laser-focused. She presented her data distinctly and answered exactly what she was asked. Then she thanked the committee, the audience, and rested her defense.

There was a brief break while the committee left the conference room. Caren stepped out as well while Nikki and Chance shot each other a look—their hearts in their throats. This was it. Caren either passed or failed. She had a future at the University of Michigan, or she didn't.

A short while later, a committee member stepped out to tell Caren to return to the room.

"Congratulations, *Dr.* Michelson! That was a beautiful

defense."

Nikki collapsed at the table, releasing the breath she didn't know she'd held, and let loose a long whistle that shook the staid halls of the university. People were on their feet, clapping. Rushing to her side, Nikki hugged her sister. *She did it! The ordeal is over, right?*

CHAPTER FOUR: CHEERS!

Nikki slumped in her seat. *What a relief. I was a nervous wreck.* Chance hugged Caren. "This calls for a celebration! Let's get out of here."

"I second that," Nikki agreed.

Caren seemed to be in a daze as she began closing the smart desk down and retrieving her laptop. She smiled. "I've had it. I just can't think of another thing."

Caren looked exhausted. Nikki took a breath. *We all look whipped. I'm drained*

"I made reservations for all of us at six o'clock at *Leonardo's*. We'll see you there," Chance said to Nikki.

She and Caren headed for the parking structure while Chance returned to his office, a huge smile on his face.

"What a relief," Caren said taking a restorative breath. "I am so glad that is over!"

Nikki gave her a big hug. "You can say that again. Now, we celebrate and then get busy planning your wedding! Meanwhile, I have to get back to work."

Caren waved goodbye. "I'm going home to take a nap."

The smile on Caren's face said it all when she got home. Daisy, Gus and the children cheered!

"Mommy's back!" Emily cried.

"What happened to *Dr.* Mommy?" Caren teased.

Emily giggled. "Oh yeah. *Dr.* Mommy, can we make some chocolate chip cookies?"

"How's about some lunch first?" Gus interjected. "Your mommy didn't eat much this morning, I noticed."

She just shrugged. "My stomach was too queasy to eat."

Daisy shot her a secret smile and a knowing glance. "I noticed, too, so I made homemade chicken noodle soup. Here's a nice fresh soda cracker to tide you over, Caren, until I can dish it out."

Caren was grateful for Daisy's thoughtfulness. "Just what the doctor ordered. Oh, and that would be moi." She primped and pointed to herself with pride.

Zach pulled a chair out for her. "Hey, Doc, you sit here at the head of the table."

"Where I always sit." She giggled as she allowed herself to be seated.

Daisy placed a bowl in front of her. "Here you go. This is good for whatever ails you."

Giggling Emily added, "Mommy, Gram Daisy and I made noodles—homemade!"

"Impressive."

Caren's cell rang. She grinned as she looked at the caller ID. "Dr. Michelson here. How can I help you?"

"Dr. Michelson, this is Dr. Chance Matthews. I just wanted to touch bases with you and congratulate you. What are your plans?"

She chuckled. "After a power nap, I have a doctor's appointment. I'm getting my annual Pap test and some blood work for a certain ceremony I'm scheduled to attend."

"Oh, and what might that be?"

"Hmm, if you don't know, perhaps I should rethink my immediate future," she mused.

"No need for that." He was serious now. "I just got back from my own appointment. We'll have everything we need for a license."

"Yikes! I better let Nikki know in case there are any other

hoops we have to go through."

"Good idea!"

She called Nikki at work and left a voicemail, as her line was busy. Then she went to take a short nap while Gus, Emily, and Daisy tackled making homemade chocolate chip cookies.

It wasn't long before she heard the front door open and close, and assumed Gus was taking Zach to the grocery store for the must-have, perfect, secret ingredient . . . macadamia nuts — *in honor of the occasion.* That occasion being the wedding and subsequent trip to Hawaii and of course her newly earned doctorate.

Nikki got Caren's message. The time to pay the price for her comments to Mark had come. She needed to call and have Mark work his miracles with the powers that governed weddings in Hawaii. She had no idea how that worked. Maybe she'd luck out and get his voicemail.

But, no, he answered on the first ring. "Hello, Nikki, Mr. Cad here."

"I was wondering how we'd recoup from that."

He laughed. "Consider it over. For now. What can I do for you?"

Nikki asked about the blood work and wedding license.

"Have them fax the paperwork to our office. Jane is our resident expert. It doesn't take much, two pieces of identification, proof of birth, easy things like that. They'll have to apply in person, but they can print up the wedding license application ahead of time. We actually have arranged weddings for several of our clients. Have you had time to research Hawaiian wedding traditions?"

Nikki was glad that they were back on safe and familiar ground. What did she really know firsthand about Mark? And was it her business anyway? She hung up after agreeing to call the next day about any details they needed to cover before they left for Oahu. Nikki's intercom chirped. Her next client had arrived.

Caren left the doctor's office in an even more distracted state than when she entered. Her Pap test was completed, and her blood work as well. She made a quick stop to CVS on her way home—just to be sure.

When she got home, she put the CVS bag on the table next to the other one there, then she got distracted with Emily, who was delighted to have her mother back. After talking with her and playing a bit with her Barbie Doll outfitted in an elaborate wedding gown, Caren headed for her shower.

She was about to enter the bathroom when Daisy caught up with her.

A small smile crossed Daisy's lips as she hesitated. "Dear, I think this package is for you. I thought it was my prescriptions Gus picked up, but . . . see, I have no use for this."

Caren started, grabbed the package, mumbled nothing in particular, and went to take care of business. After a refreshing shower, she joined her family to leave for their celebration dinner at *Leonardo's.*

"Dr. Caren Michelson, I presume? Follow me please," the hostess said. She led them to a small dining room where Nikki and Chance were already seated.

"Hello there, Dr. Michelson"—her sister stood to give hugs all around—"This was one big day. I, for one, am ready to par-tay."

Nikki had already ordered some Asti Spumante for that very purpose and added sparkling cider for the children. Everyone raised their glasses as person after person made their toasts. Caren was interrupted with cries of *speech, speech* so often that she left her glass untouched. Despite the chicken soup, her stomach was still unsettled.

"That must have been the longest title of a dissertation that I have ever been privileged to hear," Chance commented.

Caren laughed. "I never had time to give it a title, so my chairperson used the description in the abstract!"

"Does that mean you get to stand a long time, Mommy — oops — Dr. Mommy, when you have your gramation?"

Caren chuckled as she corrected Emily. "That's graduation, sweetie. And yes, that's exactly what it means."

"Take all the pomp and circumstance you can get, you earned every minute of it. Enjoy every single second of it," Gus counseled.

She took a deep breath. "Now, time to discuss some really important research work — "

She was interrupted by a chorus of groans across the table.

"Talk about a buzz kill," Zach grumbled.

" . . . about Hawaiian wedding traditions." Caren finished with a smile.

The relief around the table was profound as everyone released a collective sigh.

Nikki was glad Caren could now assume some responsibility for the wedding planning, giving her a much-needed chance to think. She had a few appointments to reschedule, packing to do for her early trip to Oahu, and she seriously needed to get her To-Do list in order. Nikki needed to call Mark about last-minute details concerning their flight.

Then Caren interrupted her musing. "What do you think of a barefoot wedding, Nikki? Chance?"

Chance grinned. "Fine with me, as long as we'll be on our favorite section of beach for a part of the ceremony." He shot Caren a look that made her blush.

Probably some shared memory of a heated *episode* there. Nikki made a fist bump. "Another decision down! That's what I'm talking about! Remember, *both* the bride and groom wear white. That reminds me, I have to figure out what I'll wear."

Daisy beamed. "May I suggest you wait until you get to Oahu? You're sure to find something suitable and authentic. Why, I got my wedding kimono on Oahu. I'll be wearing it again for this ceremony. What's not true for bridesmaids is true in this case. I can and will wear my dress again."

Gus puffed his chest out like a proud peacock. "I'll wear my wedding duds, too, to walk Caren down the aisle."

Emily spoke up. "What will I wear, Mommy?"

Caren thought about it for a second, raising a finger to her lips as she spoke. "I may have just the thing. I found some fabric similar to my dress, and I thought we could find a muumuu pattern in your size that we can make together"

Zach chimed in. "I can wear that Aloha shirt you brought home for me, Mom. All I'll need is some white pants and I'm good."

"You men will all need a red sash, a Hawaiian version of a cummerbund." Nikki pursed her lips. "It's definitely island-casual attire, *but* the red is for luck, and the sash is to remind everyone just how binding the marriage is."

The dinner party wore down and everyone headed for home. Once Nikki got to her place, she greeted her Candy Cat, both grateful and glad her neighbor had agreed to feed and care for her while she was gone.

Her phone rang while she was snuggled on her sofa, and she couldn't stop the smile when she saw who was calling. "Hello."

"Hello, Nikki, Mr. Nice Guy here, how did everything go today?" Mark asked.

Nikki squealed with her excitement. "She did it!" Caren passed!"

"Was there ever any doubt?"

"Yes, actually, there was. Defending a dissertation can fail. It's not a fait accompli."

"After all that coursework and research?"

"Even after that."

"All those hours of study and the cost for the coursework and they can fail a person?"

"Yup."

"Geez. About our flight, dress comfortably. The economy and the airline industry have both tanked. I got us the best connections I could, but it's going to be a very long day."

"Really? How's that."

"The airlines have discontinued their direct flights to Honolulu. You used to stop over in Minneapolis and then fly directly to Oahu. Now, we have a three-hour layover there and then fly on to Los Angeles for another three-hour layover, board still another plane and then fly six hours, and voilà we're finally there."

"Sound like we have no say in this. I'll be sure to wear something comfy. What time do we leave?"

"I hope you're a morning person, since we have an early flight on Saturday. We board at six-forty-five." Mark replied.

"Fortunately, I am, but who complains when they're off to Hawaii?"

"You'd be surprised, plenty of people do."

"Not this woman."

"Good. That's one less hassle. Can you try not to check any luggage and just go with a carry-on? That will speed things up."

"No problem." She heard the huff Mark released and smiled, pleased she was not what he'd call a *typical woman*.

"Not a whimper of protest? You're not one of those women

then?"

"One of *those* women?" Nikki teased. She knew what he was talking about but wasn't about to let him know.

"One who needs a ton of clothes for each and every occasion?"

Nikki laughed. "No, I'm not. Does that make me a traitor to my sex?"

"Not from where I sit. You're hardly that."

"It's a tropical island, what's to pack? A bathing suit, a cover-up, a few sundresses? Easy-peasy."

"How about I pick you up at say, four in the morning? Simpler if we drive together."

"Very eco-friendly, too. My condo is on the way to the airport, so it does make good sense."

"Think you can put up with my chauvinist male pig ways for a good twenty-four hours?"

"Now *that* remains to be seen."

They exchanged pertinent information and decided to email each other regarding her address, boarding passes, and the like. When she hung up, she decided maybe he was all right after all. Time would tell. A part of her liked the idea they'd have a lot of time together. Nikki began to get excited about more than just her trip.

She spent the rest of the evening planning and packing. There would be no time to spare if in less than twenty-four hours she'd be closing shop and winging her way to Hawaii.

Friday passed in a whirl of activity. She did manage to pack lightly, deciding she could always buy what she needed or forgot. As Daisy suggested, she'd shop in Oahu for her wedding wear, knowing Caren and the rest were all set in that department.

Although she took a long leisurely hot bath, sleep eluded her. She was excited and overtired. *I'll rest on the plane.* She tossed, then turned. Try as she might, Nikki was just too excited to sleep. She was going to Hawaii, the place of her never-admitted dreams. *It isn't all too good to be true, is it? I'm really going to Hawaii!*

CHAPTER FIVE: THE LONG LONG FLIGHT

Through bleary sleep-deprived eyes, Nikki decided she didn't look half bad, considering she'd had virtually no sleep. She wondered how many more years she could get away with that before nature took its toll. She took a hot bracing shower hoping she'd perk up.

Although she was very excited and didn't feel like eating, she scrambled some eggs. The practical side of her heard Gram's voice reminding her *Breakfast is the most important meal of the day*, so she ate. Pouring a second cup of coffee into a travel cup, she heard a car outside.

Moving the vertical blinds aside, she spotted Mark in a black BMW in the parking lot. *He didn't bring his Vette today.* His head and broad shoulders were outlined from the light of the car as he got out. When he came up the walk, she opened the door.

He was casually dressed in khaki cargo shorts and a blue shirt. As he made his way into her home, Candy Cat wove in and out his legs purring up a storm.

"So, this is Candy, the cat, I presume?" Mark said bending down to scratch between her ears.

In response to his touch, the cat actually rolled on her back to expose her belly for a scratch, which he obliged willingly. Usually, she went into *attack-cat* or *scaredy-cat* mode when strangers entered her territory. Shaking her head, Nikki moved aside so Mark had more room to fondle her fickle kitty. Candy Cat cozied up to her and Emily but not to strangers. *That cat is one smitten kitten.*

"What? No Aloha island wear?" she teased.

He grinned in return. "This is it. At least for now."

He looked tanned and fit. His legs with their fine dark hairs were a surprise. *Hot, and good man legs. Yowser. What a handsome hunk!* She fanned herself mentally.

He came into the living room and gave her a quick nod of approval. He must have liked her navy tube-topped sundress with a contrasting short-sleeved jacket, because a crooked smile creased his even features.

"You, on the other hand, look good enough to eat. Speaking of which, you did eat, didn't you?"

She nodded and smirked. "Yes, Mother, I did."

"Sorry." He shrugged. "Old habits die hard."

"How's that?" she asked as she poured a cup of coffee for him.

"I raised my kid sister, Mellie. You remind me of her. She's on her own now, and I still shudder to think what she's eating . . . or not eating." He set his half-finished coffee aside. "But we really need to head out now."

"Oh? Then we both raised a sister. Interesting."

"That taste of freedom after she went off to college accounts for my delayed foray toward maturity. Oh, well . . . Got everything?"

"Yup," she said setting the alarm on her door and locking it, but not before she poured some dry cat food into the dish. Fortunately, her neighbor had Nikki's alarm code and key so she could care for Candy Cat.

They made the short drive to the airport with enough time to spare. After going through the security clearance and getting stopped for extra wand waving, they walked the terminal to the escalator that took them beneath the sprawling metropolitan airport complex and through a colorful panoramic light-show tunnel with the sounds of New Age music.

"I always get a kick out of this section." Mark chuckled as

he nodded his head at the light display and stepped on the moving beltway.

Nikki grinned in return. "Very space age. I wonder what visitors think when they see it?"

They found out as some teenagers went by making eye rolls and adjusting their iPods to increase the volume, most likely to drown out any possible sound contagion.

They emerged and walked to their gateway. Finding seats, Nikki pulled out her e-reader and checked her email as Mark settled in for the hour-long wait. Time flew. When they called for first priority seating, Mark stood. Nikki looked at him questioningly.

"Premier seating, a perk of *W T and T* management."

Nikki gathered her carry-on, e-reader, and purse, then preceded him onto the plane. With a confident stride, she greeted the sky attendant and walked ahead to search for her seat, only to return the way she had come because she couldn't find it. She was confused. The sky person checked her ticket and led her to a wide, comfortable window seat next to a grinning Mark — in first class!

She was chagrinned. "Don't say a word."

Trying to look innocent, he asked, "What? *W T and T* is *world* class, and that makes *us* first class."

She settled into her luxury seat prepared to throttle him later. She knew there was nothing she could do but enjoy it, for the moment.

Unlike many people, Nikki didn't hate the take-offs and landings. She loved the roar of the engines, the sudden acceleration, the lift-off.

Mark's chiseled face paled and his hands gripped the armrests. "I hate this part. I know it's stupid, but I hate take-offs and landings."

Nikki slipped her hand in his and held tight. A surge went through her, and she was sure they were both shaken by it, because Mark looked taken aback, too.

When the plane reached cruising altitude, the hostess brought them mimosas and croissants, which Nikki surprised herself by practically inhaling. After the seatbelt sign no longer flashed, she and Mark used their tray tables to rest their tablets on. Nikki tapped her screen for her notes on the wedding plans.

"What progress have we made?" Mark asked.

"Quite a lot, actually. Thanks to you. We have the ceremony set for both the chapel and the beach at the Coconut Plaza Hotel. They put me in touch with the priest—a kahuna?" At Mark's nod, she continued, "Kahuna Kane."

"I take it Chance has taken care of the rings?"

"Yes. He had them carved from Koa wood and had both pearls and diamonds inset into the wood, then embedded the wooden rings within titanium bands."

Mark whistled. "Wow. I'd like to see that. It must have cost a pretty penny. Koa is a very sacred and special wood."

"As co-wedding planner, you'll see them, all right, since you'll be there supervising the details. Speaking of which, were you able to secure Kekoa?"

"I did. I'll firm things up with him and Jasmine when we get to Oahu."

"Jasmine?"

"She's our talented photographer that I hired for the wedding. Her cousin will do the videography, too. They have both worked with Chance and Caren."

"How's the guest list and voucher end of things going?" Nikki asked.

He shot an admiring look her way. She could tell he was impressed by her business sense, her keen mind . . . as well as her curves, no doubt.

He flashed her a half grin. "As you predicted, my dear public relations expert, people responded well. Most are coming and staying at the Plaza, and they have used their vouchers. We'll get quotes and photos from them to generate more business."

As lunch was served, they stopped and ate, chatting easily about this and that. When the reminder flashed to buckle their seatbelts and prepare for their 3-hour layover in Minneapolis, Nikki and Mark got ready to land. Once the aircraft stopped, they gathered their belongings and deplaned.

As they walked the airport terminal, Mark led them to a comfy Delta Premium Perks Customer Lounge that was spacious, offering drinks, snacks, Wi-Fi connection as well as showers. After reading for an hour or so, Nikki noticed Mark had fallen asleep. So far, their morning was going well. *We still have at least twelve hours to go.* She hoped for the best.

Nikki continued to read as the clock moved on, then roused Mark so they could make their connecting flight to Los Angeles.

"I must have dozed off," Mark apologized, recovering as they walked. "I'll need some coffee once we board."

"Since we're in first class, I'm sure that can easily be arranged."

Once they boarded and were settled, Mark automatically reached for her hand as the plane rose into the blue sky. Nikki didn't pull her hand away. *Good thing I'm here. He needs me.* The thought amused her.

"Did you have any problem getting away from work early?"

"No, I was able to move my schedule around. No big deal."

"How did your boyfriend take it? Is he meeting you there when the other guests arrive? That could translate into a very pleasant interlude."

"No, he won't be meeting up with me."

"Why on earth not? Is he nuts to pass up time with you on a tropical island?"

"No, not nuts, just non-existent."

A pleased and relieved smile crossed Mark's handsome features.

Nikki met his smile with one of her own.

"So, you are footloose and fancy-free?"

"Yes." She raised her brow. "Are you? Or do you have someone waiting? Will she be greeting you? A girl in every port? Or on every island?"

"Ouch. I date, but I'm not that bad. I don't sleep around, either."

She snickered. "You look like the classic *bad boy*."

"Didn't your mother teach you not to judge a book by its cover? Doesn't that make you guilty of reverse sexism?"

She laughed outright. "Reverse sexism? Did you just make that up?"

"If the shoe fits . . . or in this case if the words fit . . . Seriously, I wonder if that remark isn't sexual harassment or something?"

She giggled, semi-outraged at his gall. "Puh-leeze! Give me a break!"

"I dunno . . . if it walks like a duck, sounds like a duck . . . I rest my case."

She shook her head. "No comment."

"Wait a minute, let's review. It looks like we are both single and available. Am I right, or am I right?"

She was reluctant to agree. "We are. But that does not make me interested."

"Oh, but you are," he said reaching over to touch her on the arm, proving his point.

She snatched her arm away and turned her attention back to her e-reader.

He grinned like the Cheshire Cat, then closed his eyes to nap.

CHAPTER SIX: AND THE BEAT GOES ON

After several hours they landed in LA. Nikki was glad for the break. She needed to stretch. Once again, they sought out the similarly equipped World Perks Lounge, grabbing some juice and snacks in preparation for the 3-hour layover.

Nikki spent some time people-watching, as flyers from all over the country frequented the lounge. It was a way to pass the time.

She found herself growing restless, though, and left Mark to walk the terminal for a bit to get a break from the tedium of waiting. Not for the first time, she wished she could doze as easily as others, but she was not one of those fortunate ones.

She browsed in a few shops along the way, then returned to the lounge. The wait was beginning to wear on her, and there was still a 6-hour flight across the Pacific. She still had to pinch herself to accept that this was real and she was winging her way to Hawaii. Mark was still dozing when she returned to his side.

Using her e-reader game function, she occupied herself by playing Scrabble against the computer. She was chagrined when she lost. *Must be a set up like the slot machines in Vegas.*

She roused Mark so he could freshen up before their final flight. Using the women's restroom to splash some cold water on her face, she perked up and reapplied her makeup. Soon, she and Mark left the lounge to board the plane.

Back in first class, they were underway awhile before dinner was served. Nikki noted that Mark had had no alcohol whatsoever, something that a person with a problem drinking could not carry off for so long, especially when alcohol was so easily procured. She breathed a mental sigh of relief. *Not expecting much from my too charming companion or anything.*

Considering it was airline food, the meal was acceptable, and it did make them both feel better. Mark set his roll onto Nikki's tray. She raised an eyebrow appreciatively and smiled her thanks.

A flush stained his cheeks. "What? I can't be a nice guy? I noticed you like bread."

"Did I say anything?" she asked buttering the roll.

He gave her a wink and returned to his meal.

"Do Chance and Caren want anything crazy? For the wedding, I mean . . ."

"Like what?"

"I don't know . . . zip lining into the chapel?"

She giggled. "No."

"Arriving on dolphin backs?"

"Nope."

"Dogsled?"

"Oh, for heaven's sake. Where are you getting these ideas? Is that what you'd do?"

He grew silent for a minute, thinking. "No, I'd want it on the beach. On a night with a full moon. And as long as I was doing it, I'd want to exchange leis before we exchanged rings."

"That's a lovely idea! Let's build that in."

"The groom's lei should be maile leaves. It's tradition."

"Is it for luck like just about everything else?"

A knowing glint sparkled in his eyes, "No, it's for fertility."

"Seriously?"

"No. I made that up, but it is used to communicate love, enduring devotion, and a desire for peace. Nothin' to do with fertility."

"Good. Otherwise, my groom couldn't wear them."

"What no kids?"

"Now, did I say that?"

"Well, no. But . . ."

"I think adoption is more my thing. I'm pursuing it."

"Seriously? Because you don't want to ruin that beautiful body, huh?"

She smiled. "I just have a soft spot for children stuck in the system. If I had a loving family to offer, that's what I'd do. Maybe I'll be considered enough family, who knows."

"Hmm, I like kids. Adoption's fine, I guess. Kind of always took having them for granted."

"It is possible to adopt a baby, if you like."

"True, either way, fine with me." He smiled happily as he finished the last of his pineapple sorbet.

They spent the next ninety minutes watching the feature-length movie, *Despicable Me*, then Mark adjusted his seat and promptly fell asleep.

Unfortunately, Nikki still was unable to doze. She wasn't sure if it was all the feelings she had churning inside from Mark's nearness, the fact that she was overtired, or just plain contrary. *Am I some sort of heretofore undiscovered control freak who will not let go*? She was too tired to figure it out and closed her eyes to sleep, but sleep still did not come.

Finally, she faced the truth of it. She was simply thrilled beyond belief to be going to Hawaii, and it was okay for Nicole Marie Nolan to be excited like anyone else would be. She winced from having called herself Nicole. After all, she hadn't let Mark get away with it but . . . oh well. *Oh, hell, so what if I can't sleep. I have my whole life to sleep.*

At long last, the lights came on, the captain announced they'd be landing at Honolulu International Airport in twenty minutes, and the cabin attendants passed out hot towels and lemons. Nikki decided that was one luxury alone that made first class, well, first class.

She gratefully used the lemon and towel but was still

somewhat foggy, disoriented, and clearly exhausted. In no time, they were deplaning. They'd left Michigan in the early morning hours, and it was very early morning in Oahu. They'd left in the dark, and they arrived in the dark.

W T and T had a Roberts Tour van arranged to transport them to the Moana Hotel. Mark had to nearly pour Nikki into the vehicle, she was that fatigued.

"This jet lag is unbelievable," she mumbled, accepting Mark's help as he fastened her seat belt. Her fingers just refused to work, and she couldn't see the clip and didn't care. She simply wanted to lie down and stop the world from spinning. The lack of sleep was taking its toll. Even the excitement couldn't keep her going much longer. "What's the matter with me?" she cried.

"Nothing that bed won't cure," Mark assured her.

"Ha, Ha. Very funny."

"No, I'm serious, you've been up twenty-four hours, and there's a six-hour time change. The flight by itself is bad enough, but the layovers are a bitch. You're zapped from it all. The ride to the Moana is about thirty minutes."

Nikki found herself falling to the side and bumping Mark as she dozed in fits and starts. Finally, she quit trying to fight off the sleep and gave in.

She woke with a start realizing her head was resting on Mark. *So what? He's not complaining. Can't a girl take comfort where she can? Besides, this proves once and for all I'm immune to Mark's charms and his touch.* Surprising herself, Nikki stayed where she was. Her head slipped to rest on his chest.

Mark thoroughly enjoyed the moment of connection with Nikki. A rush of tender feelings made him feel protective, a feeling he was not accustomed to, but one he found he could learn to like. He was pleased with himself, because during his time with Nikki he discovered he was adapting easily to no more late nights carousing, and his drinking was no issue. He no longer felt the need. Any urges he experienced were caused by Nikki, not alcohol.

The Moana was the last hotel on Waikiki Beach, yet it was the first hotel to be built on the island. Mark imagined Nikki would enjoy its history as well as its ambiance and luxury. When they arrived, he carefully eased himself from Nikki and woke her gently, then settled up with the driver.

Noticing Nikki was following him like a dazed, completely worn-out puppy, he'd bet she was feeling lightheaded and dizzy, too. How she shuffled along made him think of his own past hangovers and jet lag, yet neither of them had anything to drink the whole day.

It was two in the morning when the bellhop showed them to their rooms. They were on the 5th floor. Mark's room was next to Nikki's, but he followed her into her room as the helpful bellhop placed her suitcase on the luggage stand.

Giving them a fast tour of the room's amenities, the bellhop opened the lanai door to let in the gentle tropical breezes and left. In the background, the sound of the sea surging in and out provided a lullaby. Nikki swayed on her feet with fatigue and brushed the bedside Vanda orchid and gold foiled candy aside as she stepped out of her slides. Mark dimmed the bedside lamp.

Then before she could protest, Mark turned her around so her back faced him. In one smooth move, he whisked her skimpy sundress up and over her head. He noted her shapely hips resplendent in a scrap of lace thong. He deftly maneuvered her into the bed. As he did, he was shocked to see a tattoo on the small of her back.

He muttered and smothered a moan. "Nikki, Nikki, aren't you a surprise."

He really needed to get a closer look at that tattoo, he decided, but not now, not like this. As she slid into the bed, he couldn't help but notice the tattoo was neither too large nor too small, and it appeared to be an angel. *You little devil.*

He continued to be a perfect gentleman. He had deliberately positioned Nikki's back to him when he removed her dress because he had determined earlier she was braless. Standing behind her, he could not *see* her breasts, but he'd already decided they were nicely shaped and full. It wasn't his doing she wore a thong and he saw more than he'd bargained for. He was certain that if Nikki were not in an altered state of mind, she'd have had his head by now. *She wouldn't be very comfortable sleeping in her tight sundress, now would she?*

When Nikki awoke, she was famished . . . and half naked! She vaguely remembered her dress being removed, but that was it. There was nothing she could do about it, so she dismissed it from her mind. There were more exciting things to think about like her wonderful room. No, make that suite!

It was luxuriously appointed with a chaise lounge set by the door wall. She was impressed beyond belief. Her room overlooked the rolling aqua Pacific. The floor-to-ceiling window on her left looked out onto Diamond Head. Ahead of her, the hotel's beautiful and lush grounds led to the ocean. She couldn't wait to explore her surroundings. Showering quickly, she dressed in capris and floral top.

She decided to take the gracious staircase down instead of the elevator. Each level had a different motif, the floors a dark hardwood. The hotel itself had been built at the turn of the century with carved banisters, cornices, and tall white colonial pillars. The lobby took her breath away. It was exquisite, a host to paintings of island venues. There were tropical trees and flowers everywhere.

She loved the open-air ambiance of the hotel. As she explored, she found herself outside a restaurant called *The Veranda.* She decided to eat there at one of the white canvas umbrella tables. It appeared that the *white* theme was carried throughout the beautiful resort hotel.

A young waitperson greeted her with a hearty *Aloha* and handed her a tall menu.

She ordered a rich cup of Kona coffee and scrambled eggs. After a moment's hesitation, she added sourdough toast with fresh pineapple preserves and went to gourmet heaven. There was fresh pineapple already at her table, along with fresh squeezed orange juice. Her view was spectacular. From where she sat, she could see Diamond Head reaching out into the blue Pacific. Long slow waves curled oh so leisurely into shore. *I can get used to this!* Before she had finished her coffee, Mark had spotted her, and with a slow smile, he joined her at her table.

"Up and at 'em, I see." He sat beside her, allowing him to savor the ocean view, too. "How do you like *The Veranda*? Not only is their food good, the view excellent, but they have live music playing throughout the night. There's even dancing at the *Banyan Bar*."

She smiled and returned his greeting. She had every reason to beam. After all, she was in paradise with a handsome and entertaining man. She was willing to give Mark a break after he'd taken such painstaking care of her during the flight over and the subsequent drive to the hotel.

"How did you sleep?" he asked

"Very well." She shook her head, bemused. "I have never been so out of it."

A teasing glint lit his eyes. "A long flight, a series of layovers, excitement, not to mention stimulating company will do that to a person."

She giggled recalling his naps. She was genuinely enjoying his banter. It spiced things up. Her excitement, long delayed, was given full rein. "Do you have an agenda for today?"

"Since its Sunday, I'm not going into our branch office of

course. But I thought we could check out the singer at *The Hat Check Lounge* this evening. Maybe have dinner. See what you think . . . In the meantime, you can use the beach, tour the grounds or shop."

"I thought I'd catch the hotel church service first. Then I definitely need to shop for a muumuu for the wedding. It's traditional wear."

"It is, but it'd be a real shame to hide your beautiful body under all that material. Why don't you consider wearing a sarong? That's popular here."

"I *do* love to shop," she repeated. Inside, Nikki was delighted at his choice of words, *beautiful body* indeed! *Fancy that, a man who likes curves . . . my curves, to be specific.* The smile on her face grew. She felt feminine, pretty, and delighted to be in Hawaii. She was filled with a soul-deep sense of well- being, her fatigue and jet lag a thing of the past.

He looked at her, his tone serious yet mellow. "Be sure to stroll through the grounds. Get a lay of the land. This really is a beaut of a location."

"Good idea."

"I'm full of them."

"I could go with the *full of it* opening you gave me, but it's too easy!"

"There are plenty of shops." He grinned as he slyly changed the subject.

"That there are! It appears to be upscale, from I what I saw." Nikki thought of her wallet.

"In this hotel, yes, but once you get outside the grounds and onto the street, you'll find every price range imaginable. Oh, by the way, don't go through the *International Marketplace* alone, okay? That's a bit risky. If you're interested, we'll do it sometime before we leave Oahu. I don't want you to experience any Hawaiian crime."

"Crime here? In paradise?"

"Here, too. Remember, even Eden had a snake. Don't you watch *Hawaii Five-0?*"

She nodded her understanding, promising not to venture there. Nikki was anything but foolish. She'd take no risks, even if it did look like heaven on earth.

"What do you say, I meet you here in the lobby, about six? We'll go to *The Hat Check Lounge.* Check out TJ and the Sharks. Catch some dinner. Dance a little."

"Dance a little?"

"I want to see how you'll fit in my arms." He smiled, then added, "For the official Wedding Planner Dance at the reception. I'm sure there'll be one, won't there?"

"Not if I can help it." Nikki laughed at his expression. "Six-ish would be fine," she said, answering his original question.

She left Mark at the restaurant, taking the elevator to the top floor of the Moana where the chapel was located. *What a view, the perfect venue for a wedding . . .* If she were to marry, she'd want it to be held here in this room of white-wood-trimmed windows overlooking the tropical paradise below.

She found it easy to worship when surrounded by such beauty. Plato thought Earth was modeled after Heaven. In her view, Hawaii's beauty proved his theory. Hawaii was Mother Nature at her finest. *Hawaii is God-perfect.*

Dreamy and haunting Hawaiian music was part of the service. Its tone added an extra touch that most stateside Sunday services lacked.

Mark entered the chapel a bit later and stood in the background just inside the door. Nikki's head was bowed in prayer.

He found time to thank heaven. Only he was thinking of the beauty and wonder of the *woman* who was beginning to capture his heart if not his soul. She was funny, smart, and pretty. He wanted her — wanted *more* with her. More of what he wasn't sure, but he knew he wanted her to be his.

He snuck a peek at her and noticed the silent tears that flowed unheeded down her face. He knew how she felt. Hawaii had that effect on him as well. He was fairly certain that Nikki could move even *him* to tears as well. He left before she did, giving her privacy.

After the service, Nikki wandered through the picturesque hotel. She marveled at the scenic paintings, carefully tended grounds, and huge tropical flower arrangements that were everywhere. Historical artifacts were carefully placed throughout the hotel, illustrating events from its long history on the island.

Later, I'll check them out. I wonder. Did Mark select this hotel based on my interest in the details of the Mauna Loa at home? Did he see I was into its history as well as its beauty? If so, wow! More kudos to him and his taste. Hmmm, if I'm not mistaken, his taste's running to me as well. He was beginning to grow on her. She tucked that thought away with a small secret smile.

She wasn't tempted to the shops yet, but she was drawn to the open-air verandas, because she loved the soft feel of the trade winds blowing against her skin, keeping the heat at bay. There was no humidity, and the temperature was perfect.

Throughout the hotel, comfortable rattan and bamboo furnishings invited guests to sit and simply be — savor the atmosphere and just *hang loose* as she had heard Chance say more than once since their trip last spring.

First things first. As Nikki wove her way through the elegant but comfortable lobby and emerged on the street, she turned to her left and began walking, relishing the island atmosphere as she canvassed the shops.

She arrived at the Royal Hawaiian Shopping Center and stopped a few minutes to watch a hula dance the students from Brigham Young University were performing to lure tourists into the Polynesian Cultural Center. A kiosk to buy tickets to the show was nearby. *Now that is worth a visit.* It would take their wedding ceremony research beyond Google. She'd be sure to mention that to Mark.

A window display behind the dancers caught her eye and Nikki entered the shop. A young Asian woman approached to help her.

"I need something appropriate and affordable for an authentic wedding on the island."

"We sell a lot of that. Size 16?"

"On a good day . . . a very, very good day." Soon she was surrounded by a variety of selections. None were working for her. She sighed in dismay, then asked, "Do you carry sarongs?"

"That would be perfect for your figure," the shop girl gushed. "Why didn't I think of that?" She rushed off to gather an armful.

Forty-five frustrating minutes later, Nikki finally found an embroidered ivory silk sarong. She turned to view herself at all angles, checking how it looked on her. The sarong lengthened and slenderized her full figure. She liked it. *Mark would approve . . . Hmmm, I'm having a hard time getting that hunk out of my thoughts.* Happy with her purchase — and the size of her new dress — Nikki walked back to the hotel.

Since they had arrived so late the night before, Nikki didn't really get a good look at the Moana Hotel from the outside until now. She gasped. It looked like someone had taken a colonial from old Boston and dropped it gently amid the graceful palms that bowed and curtsied in the trade winds. If a building could be compared to a cake, this would be a multi-tiered wedding cake.

Made of white wood with tall white columns, it boasted a curving drive with a portico. There were rocking chairs set across the wide veranda in front of the hotel. If luxury had a look, this was it, with a capital *L*. If it wasn't already much too late, she'd call Mark to change Caren and Chance's wedding venue right this minute!

She decided she would have her own wedding here. She'd use the chapel, and then to keep Mark happy, she'd plan an ocean-side exchange of leis.

Her thoughts shocked her silly, and she froze. *Whoa! Where did that come from?* More flustered and confused than she had ever been, Nikki ran into the Moana as if she could outrun her renegade heart.

Entering the lobby, she quickly ducked into a small sundry shop and purchased some strong sunscreen—both she and Caren had fair skin that was no match for the tropical sun. The stop also gave her a moment to calm her panic. Then to stay fit, and a svelte size 16, she took the stairs to her suite.

Chapter Seven: Getting to Know You

Reaching her suite, Nikki went to the windows and drew the white sheers across their expanse while she changed into her swimsuit. It was a one-piece with slenderizing side panels and an electric lime front piece that flattered her figure. She grabbed her beach tote, sunglasses, and e-reader and went in search of the pool.

She made herself comfortable poolside and started to read. She could see the ocean from her lounge chair. *Perfect view, perfect everything.* When she got too warm, she slowly entered the pool, wincing a little as the water cooled her sun-kissed skin. She dipped herself carefully into the water to enjoy the experience.

After a while, she stopped the hostess who circulated taking orders for both drinks and food. She was glad to find a lounge chair with an umbrella table to relax and enjoy her meal.

After lunch, she donned her cover-up and walked to the beach. A brief walk from the Moana was a reef-rimmed section of beach where she waded in the gentle surf. The lava reefs some hundred yards or more out protected the beach from the larger ocean swells, so the waves slowed as they reached her feet.

She noticed many mothers were swimming with their small children safely in tow. Even though she didn't swim, she felt comfortable enough to venture waist deep into the water and let the sea lift her only to drop her back in place. It wasn't strong enough to carry her into deeper water.

The water was warm and wonderful. Nikki tipped her face up to the sun and breathed a quiet prayer of thanks for this beautiful experience. If not for Caren's wedding, she wasn't sure she'd have ever traveled there.

Since she was on the sunny side of forty, she wasn't sure if she'd want to be in Hawaii alone as a single woman. Would she feel out of place in this romantic spot? Then she laughed. She *was* single and knew in her soul she belonged here. It was like coming home. The idyllic island did not make her feel left out or alone. It must be that spirit of Aloha, love, engulfing those who came to this tropical splendor.

She frolicked in the surf a bit and then walked back to the Moana. Once there, she found a helpful pool boy with a physique to pant over to relocate her on the beach. She stretched out on her stomach comfortably, hoping to doze.

Suddenly, she was lifted by a pair of strong arms. Held in place against a well-muscled chest. Mark quickly headed to the ocean with her in his arms. Still subject to his caveman moves, she screamed and pummeled him with her fists to no avail. "Put me down, you big oaf," she ordered. "I can't frickin' swim!"

He was so surprised, he dropped her. Unfortunately, the water was over her head. Immediately he picked her up and held her trembling body close to his. After she stopped shaking, he loosened his hold, and she slid down the hard length of him in relief, clinging to his body like a tree frog. He staggered back and got them to shallow water. On firmer ground, he bent his head and stole a kiss.

Gasping, she pushed him away from her, slugging him hard in the chest in the process. "You arrogant arse, what in the world? Are you trying to drown me?"

"Who knew you don't know how to swim? Who comes to

the ocean and doesn't swim?"

She pushed herself out of his arms and frowned. "Maybe someone who, I don't know, lives in Ann Arbor, Michigan. Where there is no ocean!" With that remark, she fought the surf back to the beach. That was no easy task, as the surge was stronger the closer to shore she got. It battered her as she struggled to step out. Once on the beach, she tried to turn on her barefoot heel to flounce off with as much dignity as she could muster. The sand made walking difficult, though. It wasn't easy to *flounce* in the sand.

"See you at six. I really am sorry. I just didn't know." He looked like a small boy who seriously messed up and knew it.

Her heart softened as she met his gaze. But she still stomped off anyway.

CHAPTER EIGHT: SIGHTS AND SOUND

A little less seriously ticked off, Nikki went to her suite and ordered a Mai Tai from room service. She had earned it! Changing out of her wet suit, she donned the thick bathrobe the hotel provided. She carried her drink out to her balcony lanai and sat sipping as she watched the *curlers* on their way into the shore. She knew mid-easterners called waves like that *rollers*, but here they were less fierce, less intense, so for her, they were simply *curlers*.

The more she sipped her Mai Tai, the more she calmed. She was glad Mark had introduced her to this strong fare. She needed it. She retrieved her e-reader and read until it was time for her to get ready to meet him in the lobby.

Finished with her Mai Tai, Nikki got dressed in her floral and black lace-up dress. Her breast spilled over the top enticingly, and she knew it. She had her own version of a *revenge dress. Princess Diana had nuthin' on me.* She added a flower behind her right ear and slipped on clear mule heels with a bright red flower perched over the toes. Carrying a black crocheted shoulder bag, she went to the lobby to meet Mark.

Mark had spent the remainder of the day scurrying to find a red rose to use to convey his regret regarding Nikki's ordeal. He called everywhere. It seems that while every conceivable flower grew in Hawaii, roses were not easy to get. When he found one, he had it specially delivered to her suite.

He relaxed on the lobby's veranda to await her. He wore

black dress casual slacks with a white-flowered *Magnum, P.I.* style Aloha shirt, and a white Panama hat covered his dark hair.

Mark thought Nikki was a vision as he watched her descend the staircase. He noted appreciatively how her skin was beginning to tan and how the pink tops of her full breasts strained the lace-up dress. He itched to kiss the skin above those laces.

"You really didn't have to send that lovely rose, but I'm glad you did. It's beautiful and very sweet of you."

"Did it work? My peace offering?"

Chuckling, she assured him that it did, and they left it at that.

"You look fabulous." He winked, looking her over appreciatively. "Very nice." He touched the small of her back guiding her through the lobby.

He felt Nikki respond with a frisson of excitement at his touch. He recalled her response to their kiss and could barely wait to repeat it.

The restaurant was a short walk across the street. They passed the International Marketplace on their way.

"Would you like to take a peek at this while we're here? We have some time," Mark asked.

She nodded, a large smile crossing her face. "Just a peek."

Street vendors milled outside the Marketplace. Several performers hawked their talents. One fellow had a variety of tropical birds perching on people's shoulders while their photos were taken. On a whim, Nikki and Mark posed with three parrots, a toucan, and a very verbal Macaw. They laughed when they saw their picture. Nikki had a crazed look on her face while he had a cockeyed grimace as he tried to engage the toucan on his arm. They each bought a copy of the souvenir photo.

They entered through an archway trimmed in ivy and

tropical flowers. The place reminded Mark of a colorful, large flea market. People from all over the world displayed their wares and shopped their crowded aisle-ways. Carts and kiosks held a treasure trove.

He held up a finger in warning. "Be careful not to stand too long in any one place, or you will be hounded—"

"Too late!" Nikki said as she was snagged by a wiry Asian man who promised to give her not one but two different *natural shell* necklaces for twenty *dolla*.

When Nikki tried to put them back on the rack, the vendor countered, "For you, wahine, fifteen dolla. Good buy. You like it." Nikki intended to walk away when the man turned to him. "You get for her. Only ten dolla."

Mark—cocking an eye at Nikki to see if she wanted them—paid the man. "Which one would you like to wear?" He held one up, offering to put it on her.

Nikki turned so it would be easier to work the clasp. When his touch grazed her skin, he noticed her response with satisfaction. *Not attracted to me, huh?* His touch seemed to send goosebumps down her neck and shoulders. He hoped his touch registered deep within her. Her warm, soft skin certainly aroused him.

Mark and Nikki had not gone into the Marketplace very far before they came to the huge banyan tree. Its heavy-laden branches provided a roof over the courtyard. Even there, rows upon rows of merchandise beckoned.

An elaborately made-up woman in a sarong—with a slit in the side that stopped way north of her thigh—looked at Mark with a hint and promise of more to come if he so desired. Mark caught sight of Nikki's frown. *Ha! She noticed and didn't like what she saw.* That much was clear.

The woman went to the weeping banyan tree and drew its leafy limbs aside, revealing a small series of rooms. Christmas lights were strung around the tree itself as well as the adjacent kiosks. It looked pretty but also somewhat sinister . . . eerie. The woman squeezed past Mark close enough for her breasts to touch him. As she passed, she slipped a small card into his shirt pocket.

The crowd seemed to grow. Pressed by the people, Nikki gripped her purse tightly and leaned toward him. "Do you mind if we leave now? It's so congested and cramped. I'm usually not claustrophobic, but . . . I *am* ready to leave."

"Don't mind in the least," Mark said as he wound the two of them through the maze. "See why I don't think it's a good idea to be here alone?"

Mark took her hand and gently pulled her through the throng. When they emerged onto the street, the archway of ivy and flowers moved. Not an arch at all, but a cleverly costumed person contorted to look just like an archway. They laughed as the *archway* lit a cigarette.

"Sure had me fooled," Mark commented.

They had tarried in the Marketplace longer than Mark had intended. It was dark already. Night fell fast in the tropics. There was no gentle glooming—it was day and then it wasn't.

A few curious cats with kittens wound their way through their ankles, but neither Nikki nor Mark stopped to play with them. They continued walking, paying homage to the white-faced mimes, the street musicians, and faux statues that were cleverly camouflaged people. Soon they reached their destination.

Mark hoped Nikki liked *The Hat Check Lounge* and its circa 1940 art deco décor. It featured an area for the small band scheduled to play soon. There was a dance floor, too.

Linen table cloths covered the small round tables set intimately throughout the room. A lit candle in a red bowl centered on each table set an intimate atmosphere. There was even a cigarette girl circulating with her box tray. Mark knew she also delivered drinks, so he flagged her so they could order drinks.

When they were alone, Mark set his elbows on the table. "TJ is scheduled to play tonight, and Jasmine takes photos of tourists here when she is not on assignment with *W T and T.* I've already talked with them via phone, and both are interested in working the wedding. I can vouch for them."

"This will be fun! I've heard Chance and Gus carry on and on about this place. Daisy loved it, too. What type of music does he play?"

"See for yourself." He nodded toward the stage as a tall, well-built man approached the mike and introduced himself and The Sharks.

TJ was slim, tall, and blond. He looked like a surfer. His skin was golden, his long locks bleached in the sun as if he had had professional highlights added. He wore island-casual as did his bandmates. They began playing. Listening as their dinner arrived, Mark and Nikki talked in between bites.

"I bet you bring all the girls here," Nikki smirked.

He shrugged, careful to maintain a casual tone. "Not all, but I do like this place."

"Very slick, Mr. Mark. So far, the music is fantastic. Big Band fits this venue to a T."

Mark was pleased with her assessment. "But can people dance to it?"

Nikki looked around and gave a small laugh. "People are up and dancing."

"But not you."

"He hasn't played my favorites yet."

Mark coaxed them out of her, then waved the waitperson over and whispered the titles. "Ask TJ to play these as a favor to see if they'll work for the wedding we're planning." He slipped a folded bill along with his requests into the young server's hand.

"That's cheating."

"How else will we know if he can do what we need? You'll want to dance at the wedding, I presume, so let's make sure he can do justice to your requests. This is research." He led Nikki to the floor as the band tuned up.

TJ announced, "Ladies and Gents, we're going to jump several decades to try some special requests for a wedding couple over here"—he gestured to Nikki and Mark—"so with your indulgence, we're going to step it up for two songs after *Blue Moon*."

Nikki began to protest when a spotlight singled them out as if they were the wedding couple.

Mark chuckled. "Give it up. It'll be worse if we try to correct him."

He held her as closely as he dared when they began to dance. The music was dreamy and romantic. He felt her resistance melt as she leaned into him. Too soon, the song ended, and the band broke the tension building between them by launching into a rousing *Proud Mary*.

Looking at him she whispered, "Cheater," then began to rock and roll.

No sooner had TJ finished her selection than the band launched into *Jeremiah Was A Bull Frog*.

Mark yelped. *"Jeremiah Was A Bull Frog!* Jesus! Back to back with *Proud Mary?"*

She shrugged her shoulders. "You asked for it!"

"So I did." They were both out of breath when the tempo changed to mellow *Blue Hawaii*.

He whispered into her ear as he gathered her body closer. "No one said I couldn't put in a request or two of my own."

He liked the feeling of being pressed heart to heart as he guided her across the dance floor. He breathed in the gardenia scent she wore and found it oddly stirring. He led her out onto the patio, where they danced in the moonlight. There was a full moon, and the trade winds caressed them as they held each other. He tipped her head and lifted her chin as he kissed her lips with *Blue Bayou* playing in the background. He led her back to their table when the band took a break.

TJ joined them to seal the deal. "This will be one awesome gig," he said. "Happy to oblige. See you Tuesday at sunset. Coconut Plaza Hotel on Kauai, right?"

Mark confirmed with a nod and a smile.

Soon after, Jasmine made her way over showing them some of the photos she had taken that night. "Let me get one of you two." She snapped a quick shot, then brokered her deal and agreed to shoot the wedding photos.

Nikki and Mark left the restaurant. Holding her hand, he led Nikki through the Royal Hawaiian Shopping Center until they reached the gardens of the famous Royal Hawaiian Hotel.

"I can't believe this shopping center hides these beautiful grounds, this wonderland. No one would know the hotel was behind a shopping center," Nikki murmured.

The grounds were impressive with their manicured lawns giving the illusion of a tropical paradise. The long garden pathway wound its way amid lush flowers, palm trees, and ferns, with tiki torches lighting the path. They reached the seaside piano bar and sat at a table lit by a candle holder shaped like the Pink Palace, as the locals called it. The building was Moroccan in style with walls of pink stone.

"Now, let's get you a real Mai Tai. Some say the original was created here."

"When my sister stayed here, she said she wanted to taste every known tropical drink."

His tone deepened. "And you? What do you want to taste?"

Nikki leaned over and planted a gentle kiss on his lips. It seemed she wanted more but stopped herself. "More, of this," she said. Breaking the spell, with a telltale glint in her eye and an impish grin, she went on to say, "Believe it or not, I want to sample Hawaiian desserts."

"Say what?"

"Oh, I dunno. Baked Hawaiian, maybe."

"Seriously?"

She cocked her head. "Coconut Cake, Hula Pie, Pineapple Upside-down Cake . . . Need I go on?"

"You can, but I get the gist. The Pink Palace has a mean Macadamia Nut Cream Pie. You game?"

"Yes! Too bad it'll go right to my hips."

He waggled his eyebrows. "I should hope so!" Giving her a heated look, he added, "It could go to . . . uh . . . another place or two."

Nikki caught his drift and smiled.

"Actually, I like a woman with a little meat on her bones. I find you very attractive."

"Well, that seals the deal, Macadamia Nut Cream Pie it is."

They put their order in. When it arrived, it was artfully presented. It boasted not only meringue but fresh whipped cream.

"Not to worry, we can find ways to handle anything that comes along be it food, drinks, desserts . . . we can find ways to work it off." He smiled as he took a bite of the pie.

Nikki raised an eyebrow. "Here comes the hit! I'm not going there, so I won't ask how."

"If you had, I'd say, let's hike Diamond Head tomorrow. While we're here, we might as well see a little of the sights. This trip doesn't have to be all work. But speaking of work, you gave me an idea with all your dessert talk. Why don't we consider a dessert buffet for the reception in addition to the wedding cake? Then, when we indulge, it's simply *research*."

"My hero," she purred taking another bite of the succulent pie. "Mmm, we can have a tier of Hawaiian themed cupcakes, too, in a variety of flavors. Oh, and they can be decorated with

Hawaiian flowers, sea shells, sea stars!"

"I never thought I'd say this—I never imagined I'd be a wedding planner either—but I like it! Seriously, though, while we're here, we can squeeze in a Mai Tai," Mark added.

When the drinks arrived, Nikki took a sip and moaned in delight. "Mmm, there is absolutely no comparison! I thought the Moana Loa at home had a good one, but this beats the band." She paused as they enjoyed the view from their ocean-side table. "You know Caren had asked me to scout out some activities for the kids while we're here. We have a solemn pledge to keep."

Mark smiled and nodded. He was having a hard time keeping his cool around her. "We do. Fun is officially on the agenda. We have to do what the bride requests. Actually, we have an obligation to research recreation. Game on!"

Nikki laughed. "I know!"

"After hiking Diamond Head—for the kids' sake—we'll stop at *Duke's* for Hula Pie."

"You're on."

"Then, we'll work that off by going for a long walk on the beach. In fact, when we're finished here, we'll walk the beach back to the hotel."

They left the piano bar, slipped off their shoes and walked the beach in the moonlight. Mark automatically took her hand as they walked—she didn't object.

Nikki stopped to rest about halfway. "I'm amazed at how hard walking on a beach is. It looks so easy in the movies."

"Let's move down by the ocean. The sand is firmer there. It should be easier."

He was right, the walk was easier . . . and more fun. Occasionally, a wayward wave flowed over their feet. They laughed, bobbing and weaving away as the waves chased them. They continued to stroll, soothed by the trade winds and moonlight. Neither said a word, but the silence was comfortable. The magic of the beach was enhanced by the fire of the tiki torches that lined their path.

A woman in bare feet wearing a muumuu approached them. Each of her arms was laden with leis. "A lei for your lady?"

"Yes, please," he said, selecting one made of violet orchids.

The old woman beamed and winked. "She deserves a proper island welcome."

Walking a little way from the smiling woman, Mark took the lei, then placed it over Nikki's head, kissing first one soft cheek, then the other. Then his mouth moved over her willing lips in a searing kiss. "Welcome to the Islands." He kissed her again. The kiss was deep and meant to arouse.

Nikki raised her hand to her just-kissed lips and held it there for a second as he walked her inside the hotel. "Tomorrow we hike Diamond Head. How about an early breakfast?"

"Okey-dokey." She walked off toward her suite with a soft smile on her face.

CHAPTER NINE: DIAMOND HEAD

Nikki was not confused anymore. He *wanted* to kiss her! She now knew the ocean kisses were no accident. Desire washed through her, revealing raw need and yearning. She wanted *him*.

He starred in her hot sexy dreams, where she focused on his magnificent body and thrilled at his burning touch. His ardor made his cock pulse against her dripping slit, and in her dream, she had the best climax ever.

She woke the next morning with a yearning deep inside.

True to his word, Mark called her early to announce he and a room service breakfast would be at her door in twenty minutes. They were really going to climb Diamond Head. He wasn't teasing. He took her desire to lose weight—not just maintain it—seriously. That meant something to her, and she was touched. After all, he easily could have denied she had weight to lose, even though it was in all the right places . . . mostly.

Mark arrived before the room service, a cup of rich Kona coffee in hand.

"Thank heaven," she said, accepting the heavenly blend. "Morning person though I am, I need my coffee."

Nikki was dressed in safari shorts, t-shirt, and a short-sleeved matching shirt to protect her from the sun. She was glad she had packed her running shoes, knowing she'd be darting around getting the wedding together. Mark suggested they take the stairs as a warm-up, but Nikki suspected he was giving her another chance to be fit and trim.

Once outside the hotel, Mark hailed a bicycle rickshaw to take them through the Kapiolani Park to the trailhead. The rough rickshaw ride tossed the two of them close together. Her girlie parts moistened.

Mark casually put his arm around her and winked. "To give us more room."

Nikki made no protest. Being in close confinement to his hard body was nice. She recalled the image of his rock-hard cock featured in her dreams the night before, and her blood heated.

Mark paid for their ride and asked their driver to return in 3 hours to transport them back to the hotel. They bought water from a cart located at the trailhead. Mark was wearing a fishing vest, so he placed the water bottles in the deep side pockets. "Why lug yours when I have pockets?"

"Deep pockets, I hope," she quipped. The trade winds blew, keeping them relatively comfortable as they began the climb through the vegetation. "I thought it would be a hike through lush ferns, but I'm surprised to find it more brush-like than lush."

Mark led the way. "You're in for an experience. I've made this climb before. You'll like it. It's not too strenuous."

Suddenly, she was not so sure why she was climbing a dormant volcano. True, there were plenty of others on the trail, but really climbing a volcano? *Crazy!*

"If you say so," she mumbled.

Mark set a reasonable pace, and she threw him a grateful look. Periodically, he turned to lend her a hand up a steeper section of terrain. What she knew about the man suggested he could easily make the hike a competitive man-versus-woman event, yet he didn't.

"Let's stop here for a second." He perched on a rock out-cropping, pulling her up beside him.

He handed her the water bottle. The cool liquid was

restorative. She drank, then watched as he up-ended the bottle and downed the contents. His profile, with sweat glistening on the planes of his face, made her heart race, and not from exertion either.

Nikki was pleased with herself for doing so well on the hike. "I have never climbed anything before! I think I like it."

"You'll be a pro before you know it. There's a rain forest hike we could do next. If you're game."

"Let's finish this hike first," she said. "Then we'll see . . . We do have wedding work to do, you know."

"Like what?"

"Remember the flowers? The last time I talked to Caren, she said she wanted gardenias, *green* centered daisies, and Torch Ginger for Pele and Birds of Paradise for the chapel. Oh, and as you said, a chain of maile leaves for luck."

Mark held up a hand stopping her. "Wait a minute. You lost me at Pele."

"After the volcano erupted the last time they were here, Caren's very aware of the fire goddess's need for attention. And her wrath if she doesn't get it. To pay homage to her, they are adding her flower, Torch Ginger—just in case. It's another *luck* thing."

"Why is luck such an issue for them?"

"Because they've had such bad luck. Her first marriage ended in divorce, his in death."

He nodded as he ran a hand across his forehead as if clearing his thoughts. "Makes sense. Did they have other issues? Not that those weren't enough."

"Add in Caren working on her doctorate, with two kids, dual careers, and whether they should increase their family, I'd say that's a yes."

"What do they want next? A bonfire on the beach?"

She jumped in excitement. "Brilliant idea! It can be a Hawaiian twist on the Unity Candle."

"Unity Candle?"

"You know, where the bride has a candle, the groom has a candle, they join the flames of each to a third candle signaling their union . . ."

He shrugged. "Whatever. I'm still new to all this wedding stuff. I guess we do have work to do."

"They could unite as a family over a bonfire on the beach," she gushed. "They can all have candles to light the bonfire!"

"No, each should hold a small torch. The trade winds will blow out puny candles."

"Right!" she agreed as they jumped down from the rock to the trail to continue their climb. After hiking a while, she said, "I like mixing business with pleasure." Realizing what she said she blushed.

"Me too. As much as I hate to say, *told you so* . . ." He added an innocent smile.

"Then don't."

They reached an opening in the rocky ledge when he stopped her. "It gets dark here. We need a flashlight."

"But we don't have . . ."

Before she could finish, he pulled out a small *L.L.Bean* penlight from his vest. "I was a boy scout, I am prepared."

And there's his devastating smile . . . again.

Before Mark led her into the tunnel's depths, he planted a searing kiss on her lips. He took his time and tasted her. Hearing people, he broke their kiss.

Breathless, but smiling, she quipped, "My hero." When he preened and puffed his chest out like a male mating bird would, she slugged him playfully. "Get over yourself."

"What? You'll thank me for this."

"No doubt," she muttered following him into the dark.

He was correct. Nikki was glad they had the light as they walked through the close confines of the tunnel that went straight up. It was frightening to go from sunlight to darkness in a heartbeat. Her heart beat fast, but not from exertion, rather from his passionate kiss.

She was glad Mark was there ahead of her. It was difficult to navigate this alone even with a flashlight. Then, once again, they emerged into the sunlight.

As they cleared the tunnel, they arrived at the summit. She stood in amazement at the panoramic view of ocean and sand that lay spread beneath them like something they'd find in a glossy travel brochure. Nikki froze, because the view literally stole her breath! It just didn't take her breath away. It stopped it.

Mark grabbed her hands and raised their arms high over their heads crying out, "We. Are. The. King. And. Queen." He paused to plant an enthusiastic kiss on her lips, then whispered, "Of the world."

An enterprising Hawaiian teenage boy took a picture of them doing their version of a victory dance. He gave them *the opportunity of a lifetime* to buy a t-shirt that announced, *I Survived Climbing Diamond Head*. He did a brisk business that day. Climbing Diamond Head was a feat.

Mark cocked a brow and smirked. "Imagine having his job."

"Quite an office," she agreed as they stood in wonder savoring the view.

Then he took her in his arms and kissed her soundly again. "I've never brought anyone here before . . . just you."

They spent a good thirty minutes enjoying the people, sun, surf, and view before climbing down. Mark had estimated the time of the hike correctly. When they returned to the trailhead, he whistled to the driver of the awaiting rickshaw. Nikki was tired. And hot. She sank into the seat sweating but happy.

Mark turned to the driver. "Take us to Duke's, please." At Nikki's incredulous look, he said, "What? We need nourishment. Food, drink. Hula Pie!"

She laughed, hoping it was as good as his kiss.

Nikki didn't comment further until they sat on the lanai at Duke's, where she practically inhaled the Hawaiian grown chocolate and macadamia nut ice cream dream dessert. "This is what I'm talking about." She moaned in ecstasy and took note of the look on Mark's face. *I wonder if that was how he'd look in bed if we . . .*

Mark shook his head and smiled. "You know. We have to work this dessert off."

She sighed, groaned, then agreed. "I know. I may regret asking this but . . ."

"Never fear, my dear. We'll walk the beach back to our hotel. That'll do it. But first, we have to do something about your bathing suit."

They left Duke's passing a boutique that featured swimwear.

"What's wrong with my suit? It's brand new. I got it for this trip!"

"Trust me, it covers far too much of you." He held the door to the shop open for her. "It covers your tattoo. And I, for one, would like to take a gander at that." Going to a rack, he lifted a black and red one-piece suit that was cut way low in the back and had a skimpy front too. "Try it on. You'll like it. I guarantee it."

Nikki prayed she could carry off the look. She wasn't convinced, but she tried it on anyway. Turning in the mirror, she caught sight of the tattoo and decided she did like it after all. It was a shame to hide that tattoo. It truly was a work of art.

She bought the suit, but she did not model it. Agreeing to meet on the beach — after he assured her there'd be no horseplay — they separated to change clothes and gather their beach things. They were both wearing cover-ups when they met in the lobby. Outside, Mark found a pool boy who set them up with lounge chairs on the beach.

Once they were settled, Mark turned to her with a smile. "Care to share?"

"Share what?" She could play dumb as well as the next person.

He leaned on his elbow supporting his chin. "Your tramp stamp, and its story,"

She huffed. "Tramp stamp! It's artwork, I'll have you know."

"What it is, is a crime against nature, against man, against womenkind everywhere. To keep this covered is just plain wrong."

"What? My work of art or my ass?"

"Both!" He chuckled.

She decided to tease him a bit. "Hmmm . . . I don't know . . ."

He smiled. "Whatever. I'll show you mine if you show me yours."

"Since you put it like that . . . okay."

"You first. After all, I asked first."

"Geez, how old are you? Five? Fair enough."

Nikki stood, removed her cover-up and turned to display her tattoo.

Mark wolf-whistled. "Hot damn! That is a mighty fine" — he waggled his brows — "angel. How perfectly poetic."

"Puh-leeze."

"Why an angel? Why that angel and why there?"

Nikki shrugged. "It was my twenty-first birthday —"

"And you got skunk drunk," he interrupted.

" . . . and I was with my friends, with too many Singapore Slings in my stomach . . ."

" . . . with no food."

" . . . and no food. Long story short, we decided to get tattoos."

"But that angel?"

"No wuss angel for me!" She thrust her hips out defiantly, maybe even provocatively. "This angel has the wings of Pegasus, I'll have you know."

"I like how they are spread out over both hips. Very, uh, arty. Go on."

"The body of Thor."

"Thor? Very Greek godlike of you."

"He needed to be strong and muscular . . ."

"Yes?" he prompted.

"And the face of David with an updated hair-cut."

"What's this all about?"

His fingers traced the shield that her angel held. She shivered at his touch. His caress there did a number on her insides. The look on his face told her, he felt the same.

She blushed. "It says *Halt.*"

"Why?"

"He's . . . uh . . . my Guardian Angel meant to keep me a . . . uh . . . virgin."

"And did he?"

"Did he what?"

"Preserve your virginity?"

"No comment," she responded.

"Did he at least keep the wolves at bay?"

She smiled coyly but said nothing.

"I'll file my fangs if that'll make you feel safer."

By this point, Nikki was wondering just how safe she wanted to be. After all, she was meeting what seemed to be a new man. The man Mark might really be. *Time will tell.*

"Your turn," she prodded.

Mark's face clouded. "Fair's fair." He reluctantly pulled the left side of his suit down, exposing a small heart-shaped tattoo with initials *W.W.* inside.

"At least there's no arrow through it. First love?"

"You could say that.

"Who was she? Wonder Woman?" Nikki joked to lighten the situation since Mark wasn't smiling.

"In a manner of speaking, yes. It stands for Wendy Wheaton, my mother. She died when I was twenty-one. I got my tattoo shortly thereafter in honor of the occasion, like you. Only this was my way to keep her with me wherever I went. I put it down where it wouldn't get too much attention."

"Mark, I'm so sorry." She reached out to touch the tattoo tenderly. "What a lovely tribute to her."

"Let's walk off that Hula Pie," he muttered.

Grabbing her hand, Mark led her down the beach to the section protected by the reef. True to his word, he didn't pitch her headlong into the ocean this time. Instead, they simply enjoyed the sand and surf.

"Nik," he called to catch her attention, "I've never, ever brought a woman here before, either."

Her response was to send a splash designed to wipe the smirk off his face.

They strolled back to the Moana, and Mark left soon afterward to check in at his regional office. He apparently wanted to make arrangements to get tiny fairy lights to string around the trunks of the royal palm trees on the grounds of the Coconut Plaza Hotel for the ceremony. He mentioned that after everything Chance and Caren had been through, he wanted the wedding to be picture perfect, too.

Chapter Ten: Stormy Weather

Nikki relaxed on her lanai with her e-reader and a Blue Hawaiian tropical drink. Since she and Mark had made no plans for dinner that night, she decided to try the informal dining at the *Banyan Bar*. Just as Mark had said, they did play slack-key guitar music. Not wanting to mix her drinks, she ordered another Blue Hawaiian along with an appetizer. From where she sat, once again she had a great view.

She fed the birds who visited her table in hopes of crumbs. As the evening wore on, the tiki torches were lit, and the tempo of the music changed as did the crowd. The native music gave way to a new group who played popular music.

A much younger crowd converged on the dance floor as Nikki sipped her blue concoction. She watched the largely single crowd arrive in small groups of girls and guys. As the music played, the men worked up the nerve and began to ask the women to dance. It reminded Nikki of all her high school wallflower moments. Recalling old wounds, she had felt awkward then, and just a bit uncomfortable now. *Funny how some things don't change all that much. I bet this time I'd catch Mark's eye. My off the shoulder dress would do the trick.*

Someday, she would like to find someone to love. It didn't have to be here, and it didn't have to be that night.

The tiki torches, moonlight, and Japanese lanterns made a perfect atmosphere for dancing. The full moon reflected on the sea while the trade winds kept the dancers cool and comfortable. She wished Mark were here though, but he wasn't so . . . .

Off to the side, she noticed a well-dressed, well-built man watching her. He left the corner he'd been standing in and approached her.

"Care to dance?" He sounded formal, in an old fashion, courtly manner.

Nikki was somewhat startled but recovered quickly. She rose to her feet. He held her carefully as they danced and applied his considerable charm.

"Have we met before?" he asked.

"No, I just arrived."

"We must have." He drew her closer to him. "I'm certain I saw you. Last night. In my dreams."

If this is a sample of the dating scene, I'm not missing much. Still, it was flattering to be selected from all the others there to dance in the moonlight. He was a good dancer and knew how to lead. In Nikki's experience, that was hard to find these days. She decided to enjoy his company even if he did use worn-out lines.

What's a girl like me to do but dance in the moonlight when given the chance? She threw herself into the moment, closed her eyes enjoying the gentle breeze and the mellow music. The palms danced in the wind and the music flowed over them. He smiled at her, and the way he held her told Nikki her partner was taking in her every curve. She tried to put some distance between them, but he pulled her closer. *Did my body language give him the wrong idea?*

The slow melody played on as they danced. She felt as if she were a part of a dream and he was her momentary and hypothetical dreamboat. She smiled at the thought.

"What is so amusing, chérie?" he asked.

His voice startled her out of her musing, and she blurted out the truth. "I was thinking that this must be a dream . . ."

"Does that make me your dreamboat?" He chuckled.

Her breasts were pressed against his hard chest, so close she could swim in his strong masculine scent. Her rapid heartbeat betrayed her as he whirled her about in a series of dips and complicated turns that made them stand out from the other dancers.

However, the magic of the moment was shattered when Mark tapped the man firmly on the shoulder. "Move aside, Disco Dan."

With a sad salute of defeat, Nikki's *dreamboat* sailed away with a rueful look but soon after was holding another woman.

Mark growled. "Enjoying yourself? I thought you had better taste in men."

"I was. Yes. Until you so rudely interrupted," Nikki huffed.

"I wasn't rude . . . exactly."

"At least he *asked* me to dance. I'm not marrying him, you know. It's called dancing."

"I leave you alone for one meal" — he twirled her around the dance floor — "and you let yourself be held by that player."

"Maybe I wanted to play." Her temper was rising.

A flame glowed in his eyes. "Not with him, you don't. Your angel must be having a fit!"

"You're over-reacting. Isn't this the pot calling the kettle black?"

"Look, I'm much more discriminating than you give me credit for," he countered.

"And I know this how?" She cocked an eyebrow.

"By the fact I came after you and scared him off, for your own protection and safety. You should be thanking me. You need an attitude adjustment."

"What attitude?"

"That one. The one you're having right now. You're freezing me out."

"That's because you built yourself a reputation as a player."

"Did not."

"Did so."

"You, my dear, think I hold nothing sacred, but I do. Someday I want that picket fence, two point four kids. Hell, I even want Candy Cat!"

"What?" she replied. "Do you honestly think I'll excuse your high-handed, presumptuous behavior and fall for that? You don't take anyone seriously."

Anger flashed across his face. "I do too. I take Mellie, my sister, and you very seriously!"

"So, you prove that how? By going all caveman? You're acting like a child."

"Were you leading him on?" His voice was like ice.

"What! I was simply sitting there. I didn't invite him over."

"You sure as hell didn't discourage him either."

"Are you accusing me of—"

"Using your wiles?" he finished for her. "Yes, I am. Hell, I don't know what it is about you. Do what you want. You want lover boy? Have at him. Far be it for me to stop the course of true love."

With that Mark left her stranded on the dance floor.

Nikki stomped off as well, fuming. *Men! They're assholes. Just when you forget, they go and remind you. Who does he think he is? God's gift to women? He acts as if he owns me! To hell with Mark.*

That dance had made up for her high school disappointments, and she wasn't about to apologize for it. Attending an all-girl preparatory school hadn't helped her learn about the opposite sex. She hadn't dated much in college, either. It seemed like people were already hooked up by then. What did it matter? *I don't need a man anyway, and I certainly don't want a cretin like Mark.*

Why did he have to spoil her evening? With the mellow ambiance of the evening shattered, Nikki left for her suite.

Mark fumed. *Women! They're all crazy. Hopped up on hormones and too much emotion. That's what you get when you try to protect them. That guy was a well-known sleazeball. What was Nikki thinking?* Mark found himself at the International Marketplace and looked around for a nearby bar the bar. He planned to get one big stiff drink. Hell, lots of drinks. Stuffing his hands in his pockets, he walked toward the closest bar.

He felt the business card inside where he had shoved it the last time he was there. Taking it out and reading it, he decided there were plenty of fish in the sea. He was going to find one who'd take care of something else that was also good and stiff. After several drinks, he left the bar in search of the street-walker who had given him her card.

He approached her haunts beneath the banyan umbrella tree. When he caught her attention, he noticed the glint of recognition in her eyes. She greeted him with a stroke on his groin, breathing lightly into his ear. But he wasn't responding. It wasn't that his body betrayed him or failed to work. It was something worse.

It was Nikki. He wanted Nikki, not this woman.

He knew beyond any doubt that he had acted like an igno-rant oaf at the Banyan Bar. Nikki was right. He *was* presump-tuous, and worse, possessive. Hell, he wanted her. He wanted more from her as well.

Pushing some money into the woman's hand, he left, thor-oughly out of sorts. The whole thing was entirely his fault. *I have no business interfering as if I were some kind of jealous suitor in love with my woman. Damn it, I was acting territorial.*

Stopping at the ABC store, he bought a bottle of scotch. He opened it and drank straight from the bottle once he got to his lanai.

That was where he woke up the next morning.

He sported a five o'clock shadow at noon and nursed a hangover the likes of which he never intended to have again and tried to recover from lack of sleep and a surprising lack of sanity. Downing more coffee than he had in a month, he showered, shaved and tried to salvage the day with work. He had a ton of details from his business as well as the wedding to deal with.

Nikki was amazed she was still so upset. *The nerve of the man. I can take care of myself! I always have. I know players when I see them. It was just a dance . . . one dance.* She wished there wasn't a six-hour time difference from Hawaii to Michigan. Ho Boy, she wanted to call Caren. But what could she say? That she was *p.o.'d.* Would she be any less so once she vented? Probably not.

Instead, she went on with her business of planning Caren's fairytale wedding. She busied herself by completing the seating chart. She worked on finalizing some other details, spent some time on the beach sunbathing, and had an early dinner—alone. *I don't miss Mark! I. Do. Not. Miss. Mark.*

Later that evening, she did call Caren. Once she got it all out of her system, she didn't feel much better.

"Why are you still so upset?" Caren asked. "It's not like you have to marry the man, is it? Methinks you doth protest too much. I think you like him," she sang. "I suspect something else is going on. Have you considered that Mark wasn't marking his territory as you think, but maybe he was protecting you from a known shark? And if he were, isn't that a good thing?"

"Hmph! Haven't given that a thought. It does shed a different light on it. Thanks, Caren." Since she didn't want to talk about Mark, she quickly changed the subject. "Maybe we should talk some wedding talk."

"That's more like it. Wedding talk is just what the doctor ordered."

Now what?

Chapter Eleven: All in a Day's Work

Nikki woke the next morning feeling vaguely off-center. Something was wrong, but she couldn't put her finger on it. Unless it was no Mark . . . no morning Kona coffee. How had she become so accustomed to that so fast? She was beginning to see things in a different light.

It was likely Mark was used to taking charge after his mother died. He'd raised Mellie when he was just a kid himself. He probably *did* experience a delayed wild-oats-sowing streak. She realized she wasn't being very fair about it. That, in itself, was telling.

She was about to head downstairs for breakfast when her phone buzzed. She had a text. From Mark.

Bkfst? 8?

She returned the text in the affirmative.

As she walked toward *The Veranda*, she passed the hotel florist, *Petals*, and stopped in. She couldn't find a rose to use as a peace offering, but she did spot an anthurium. *This will do.* She bought it, feeling a bit sheepish for being so prickly the night before. Maybe he was just being protective, like Caren said.

Mark was already at the table when she arrived. He stood as she was seated. He also carried an anthurium.

At the same moment, they each reached across the table

---

and exchanged flowers.

"Peace?" he asked.

"Peace."

"I ordered a pot of coffee for the table. I don't want to be *presumptuous*. I really don't. I'm such a jackass. I was totally wrong. I guess I was jealous."

Nikki nodded. "And possessive?"

"And possessive." He smiled.

"When you put it like that and bring flowers, it's really hard for me to say this, but there is an MCP issue remaining."

"MCP?"

"Male chauvinist pig."

He laughed outright at that. "I haven't heard that expression in decades! But I wouldn't go that far."

"Oh, but I would," she intoned.

With harmony restored between them, they placed their flowers in the vase containing the table flowers.

"They're in a unity vase. Long may they reign united. And let's hope for the same for us," he hinted.

"We can only hope," she responded.

He stared at her with a long slow look, then took a deep breath and released it. "Nik, the long and short of it is, I'm finding myself more and more involved with you. It scares me. Hence my boorish behavior. That's no excuse, just an explanation."

She was surprised by his confession. "I see. Will wonders ever cease?"

As they left the restaurant, Mark cleared his throat and pointed to a vehicle parked by the curb. "By the way, I've rented an SUV for today."

"What time does the family arrive?" she asked.

"At ten. I thought they would enjoy a side trip to the Polynesian Cultural Center. We can learn something and do wedding research at the same time."

She frowned, not following his line of thought. "How so?"

"Students from Bingham Young University reenact life when the ancient Polynesians crossed the ocean in their long-boats. The students are from all the islands. There are real life-sized villages, with students explaining their various cultures. It's interesting and entertaining, and we'll learn all their traditions the fun, easy way. We can also ask the villagers questions about wedding protocols."

"I think that will be an ideal excursion." Nikki smiled, then noticed the blossoms in the backseat of the SUV. "What's that back there?"

"I stopped in *Petals* and picked up leis to welcome everyone. It's tradition."

"That's kind of you. What a thoughtful thing to do." She smiled again, giving him mental kudos as well.

They got in the car and headed to the airport to pick up the family for the wedding.

"Aunt Nikki! Over here!" Emily's cries could be heard across the entire airport.

Nikki hugged and laughed with her family as they juggled carry-ons and tote bags. Gus and Mark did what heavy lifting was needed. Both she and Mark placed the leis over everyone's heads, giving each the traditional two-cheek kiss in greeting while exclaiming hearty *Alohas* in the process.

"It'll be a second honeymoon." Gus was wearing a grass hat from their last trip just a few shorts months earlier, when he and Daisy had their impromptu wedding at Fern Grotto with Caren and Chance as their witnesses. They were returning the favor for Caren and Chance's wedding.

As Nikki hugged Caren, she noticed the tears streaming down her sister's face. "Hey, I missed you too, but what is all this about? Wedding jitters?"

Chance stepped up and put an arm around Caren. He

crooned, "My sensitive girl."

Everyone piled into the deluxe SUV as Mark got behind the wheel. Lively chatter filled the car as they drove. They stopped periodically at the beautiful ocean overlooks and took pictures in every possible combination of people. Zach, Gus, Chance, and Mark tried to one-up each other mugging for the camera.

Daisy chuckled as she watched their antics. "Boys will be boys, won't they?"

When they arrived at the hotel, Mark went into his tour co-ordinator mode. "In case we get separated, let's agree to meet at the *Thatch Roof Restaurant*. I've scheduled lunch there. We'll tour the various villages. Then, we'll watch The Pageant of the Longboats."

They spent the remainder of the morning touring the authentic villages within the Polynesian Cultural Center.

"Mommy, look!" Emily cried. "He's climbing the coconut tree with his bare feet!"

The sturdy loin-clothed young Hawaiian gave pointers, and Zach and Emily were given a chance to learn about the culture. Everyone agreed the fresh coconut milk was quite tasty and all were amazed at the ancient way of life—from weaving grasses and ti leaves to pounding tapa cloth. One village prepared poi and gave out samples.

Emily grimaced."Eww! Gross. This is not as good as the pineapple we had at the last village."

Chance chuckled and ruffled her hair. "It's an acquired taste, half-pint."

Soon after, the family began to lag.

Poor Daisy looked exhausted. "I couldn't imagine doing this had we not stopped in LA for the night. That was a really good plan. Thank you, Mark."

"It's what I do for a living." He gave Daisy a brilliant smile.

Nikki knew he could have scheduled it differently and

truly appreciated what he had done for her family and the wedding.

They went to lunch and ate fresh-caught fish, hand-picked locally grown fruit, and to Nikki's delight, Pineapple Upside-down Cake. Mark caught her eye and winked at her.

He leaned over and whispered in her ear. "You did a lot of walking today. You've worked it off ahead of time."

The group strolled the grounds and came upon a chance to learn the hula. The kumus, hula teachers, were well-known for their dancing. Many took part in the island competitions.

Cocking a brow at her, Mark asked, "You game?"

"I am if you are."

"You wear authentic costumes," a young, shapely dancer said leading them off to the small thatched roofed changing stations.

Nikki wore an above the knee grass skirt, traditional coconut bra, and leis on her feet and neck. Mark's costume was a skimpy loincloth with ti leaf leis on his feet and neck.

Both Nikki and Mark were taught how to move their feet in small steps. They were a bit klutzy and were frequently out of sync, mashing each other's toes. Amid many *ows* and *oops* followed by several *sorries* they slowly began to master the dance.

The natural competition that existed between her and Mark, and recalling their previous spat, brought out the devil in them both. Everyone else paused their lessons and watched the dance progress. As the tempo increased, Nikki and Mark's movements took on the characteristics of a dual—if there was such a thing as dueling hulas, the two of them excelled at it.

She thrust her hips in a *take that* move while he parried with a sensuous *is that all you got* move. That, in turn, caused her to redouble her hip shaking.

"Care to repeat this?" she teased.

Countering her movement and squatting his knees suggestively, he said, "Oh yeah, baby."

Matching him move for move, Nikki finally gave up and surrendered. Her whole family applauded them.

"Should we repeat that performance at the wedding?" Mark asked.

"For sure," she said.

"Yes?"

"I've never done this with anyone before." She smiled wide.

After everyone finished and changed, they walked to the amphitheater to watch the Pageant of the Long Boats unfold before them. The sound of guards and drums with ukuleles and guitars accompanied the authentic reenactment. Caren was going nuts besides Nikki during the performance, whispering she absolutely had to talk to her when it was over. Nikki wondered why it was so important.

When the show ended, Caren took her aside saying, "We have to do that. It's perfect. Quick, tell Mark!"

"Hold on, Caren. Tell him what exactly?"

"Tell him that we need a long boat for Gus and me to arrive on?"

"Are you crazy?" Nikki squealed.

"No. Seriously. You haven't even seen the grounds yet. I know what I'm talking about. I've been there, and it has a long Menehune fishpond already on the grounds leading to a lagoon that goes right up to the chapel."

"Oookaaay," Nikki said. "I'll tell Mark."

The group drifted off, heading to the SUV when Nikki caught back up with Mark and told him they needed a long boat and he was in charge.

"A what?" he exclaimed. "Are you sure?"

"Yessiree," Nikki confirmed.

"This is a Caren that I don't know," Mark said. "Who knew

she was crazy? You said they don't do crazy."

"I was wrong." She laughed. "Write that down. I don't say that very often."

Mark approached Chance. "Do you feel up to driving? I have to make some phone calls to get some wedding arrangements done for your fiancée. We have a GPS, and I can guide you if you get confused, but I can't drive and use my phone. I need some time to work this out."

Chance agreed, and Mark got to work. When they reached Waikiki, Mark directed Chance to the *Pacific Towers Condominium* where he had a condo that was a short walk from the *Moana*.

Mark escorted everyone to his condo to show them around.

"Check it out, what a view!" Zach exclaimed.

As the others claimed bedrooms, Mark took Chance aside. "I booked a room for you at the *Moana*. I figure with the kids and all, you and Caren may need a place alone."

"Thanks so much. That will make it easier for Caren and the kids. She's cut me off for the duration."

"Wedding's Tuesday," Mark consoled.

"That it is."

After freshening up and recharging their batteries, the group headed out for dinner. As they walked, Zach's attention was caught by the *International Marketplace*.

"Hey, Chance," Zach called. "Can we check this place out?"

Chance glanced at Caren. At her slight nod, he turned back to Zach. "Sure, but stay close."

The group of them was soon swallowed up within the *Marketplace*. There was a lot of oohing and awing.

Daisy fell victim to a vendor while Gus was trapped in a Tiki stand with an aggressive shop owner. Caren and Chance, too, soon found themselves fending off eager vendors. Nikki and Mark walked hand in hand chuckling, having run the gambit before.

Nikki caught sight of Emily, enthralled by the huge golden koi in the pond that wound around one side of the banyan tree that covered the area. A cat with kittens stole her attention, and she tried to entice it over to her. The cat shied away. Apparently, the cat lived there but wasn't willing to put up with a little girl around her kittens. It took off in a heartbeat. Its kittens were not so experienced and lagged behind.

When Emily caught up to them, she crouched beneath some carts saying, "Here kitty, kitty. You look like my aunt's Candy Cat."

The mother returned leading her kittens, with Emily in tow, further into the *Marketplace*. Nikki didn't worry about it, figuring they wouldn't go too far.

When the family had their fill of the *Marketplace* and began walking into the restaurant, Caren turned to tell Emily to wash her hands, but she wasn't there. Because of the size of their group, they had split up. Zach, Chance, and Mark were hovering in one area while the women were hanging in another. Gus and Daisy had wandered off on their own. Seeing Emily wasn't near, Caren looked toward the men expecting to find her with Chance, but she wasn't there either.

Caren started to worry as she approached Chance. "I thought Emily was with you. Have you seen her?"

Chance frowned. "And I thought she was with you."

They stared at each other for a second, then both shouted at the same time, "Gus and Daisy!"

Caren ran into the restaurant and found Gus and Daisy at their table, but Emily was not there.

She was getting anxious now, and so was Chance.

Everyone scattered to look in the lobby and in front of the restaurant, but Emily was nowhere to be found.

Caren, close to panic, now was in tears. Chance was

consoling her when Mark and Nikki joined the upset group.

"Do you have a recent picture?" Mark asked, calmly and firmly taking charge.

Caren showed him the latest picture of Emily she had on her phone.

"I suggest you email that to all our phones so we can retrace our steps and ask if anyone has seen her," he instructed.

Caren and Chance found a policewoman and showed her photo. The young woman got the details and spoke softly into her radio while she and Chance fidgeted.

It was becoming increasingly clear to everyone that Emily had vanished.

To be continued . . .

OTHER BOOKS BY KATHY KALMAR

The Beach Series
  Beyond the Beach 1-5
  Back to the Beach Series
  Back to the Beach 1
  Back to the Beach 2
  Promises on the Beach (to be published)

The Mountain Series
  Mountain Hot (Book 1)
  Mountain Christmas (Book 2)
  Mountain Skye Prequel, the Weather Girls (Book 3)
  Mountain Joy (Book 4)
  Mountain Kiss (Book 5)
  Mountain Holly (Book 6)
  Mountain Promises (Book 7 WIP)
  Mountain Silver (Book 8 to be published)
  Mountain Mistletoe (Book 9)
  Mountain Bred, Mountain Wed (Book 10 to be published)

You may also enjoy the following from eXtasy Books Inc:

Beyond the Beach 1
Kathy Kalmar

Excerpt

"We really have to stop meeting like this, you know," he said from the floor.

Caren jerked, spilling the wine against her breasts. The red liquid spread making a large wet spot that made the thin white fabric cling. She recovered from her shock as she realized who it was. "Falling appears to be habit forming," she agreed. "Ever think of knocking?"

He winked. "What would I say? Open up, lady, you're in my pants?"

"Ah, but I'm not—" she laughed—"in your pants."

"Some thanks I get for saving your reputation."

"Seriously?"

"No offense intended, don't you think our outfits would be out of place on the World Travel van with me in my pink towel loincloth and you . . ."

She giggled. "Your towel is stunning. I think you would create a bigger stir than my t-shirt."

"Say what? Whose shirt?" He caught the fabric between his

fingers just above her throat. The huge shirt gaped and his gazes drifted to her fullness beneath. She shifted trying to step out of his grasp. As she did, the moonlight revealed the wet patch on the top.

"Looks like you didn't take very good care of it, either." His voice lowered seductively. "What's this?"

Color flooded her cheeks and her heart beat erratically as she snatched the shirt back. "You should talk bursting in here scaring me half to death and wasting a perfectly good drink in the process. Just because you look like a half-naked baboon doesn't give you the right to act like one, too."

"Baboon? Not Greek God or demi-god even? What did you expect me to do? Walk through the hotel half-dressed to your room?"

Her cheeks flamed "Uh, no . . ." Not knowing what to do, she turned to flounce off but the shoulder of the huge shirt took a dangerous slide down her arm with her movements and, as he stepped nearer to her, it slipped down her shoulder altogether.

"Lose something?" He fingered the thin cotton. She snatched at it, but he lifted it out of her reach, drawing her nearer to him.

"Stop that." She struggled to keep the too large t-shirt close around her. "What do you think you're doing anyway?"

"Trying to help." His eyes glittered as they looked at her. She could only imagine the picture she made barely dressed in his t-shirt. "That shirt you're wearing so fetchingly is mine."

"Well, pardon me." She whipped it off her body and threw it at him. "I'd rather wear nothing than something of yours." She grabbed her previously discarded dress and held it up to cover herself.

His gaze roamed the length of her. "Too late. Redheads," he paused, "even natural ones like yourself aren't supposed to wear red anyway. Ever."

"And real men aren't supposed to wear pink either, so

there."

Moments later she regretted her remark when he dropped the pink towel and strode toward her. "How right you are. Is this more preferable?" They stood there nakedly confronting each other until she, struggling not to laugh, said, "Touché." Now what?

She saw he was at a loss, as surprised as she was. Returning her bag, he found his on the bed and opened it, grabbed sweatpants, put them on and said, "Forgive me?" He stepped close to her lowering his lips to hers and kissed her.

"What are you doing?"

"Kissing you — to make it all better."

Shaking her finger at him as if he were a naughty child, she said, "You just may be incorrigible."

"Catch you in the morning," Chance said using the door this time to his room.

Caren went to the beautifully turned down bed and fiddled with a Vanda Orchid that she found on her pillow next to the chocolates. A small card lay next to it. She read the legend that a Hawaiian maiden, upon finding a Vanda Orchid on her pillow, would dream of her one true love. That night Chance A. Matthews featured in her dreams — her red-hot dreams. Uh-oh.

ABOUT THE AUTHOR

Kathy Kalmar, born in Detroit Michigan, lives with her husband, Larry in Macomb Michigan. Mother of two adult children and Grammie to three, love and family influence her writing. Like her heroine, she got her second chance to love when she married Larry in 1981. She writes non-fiction for teachers and parents and children's fiction. She reads contemporary romance and enjoys writing them. Living through her own second chance love qualifies her to write in the romance genre. She prefers to write in her Smoky Mountain cabin in Tennessee which is being rebuilt after the Chimney 2 wildfire of 2016. Although she enjoys reading, walking, and writing, she excels in hot-tubbing and in sampling chocolate and sipping generous glasses of wine preferably on Waikiki Beach. She also enjoys The Great Smoky Mountains while sitting a spell sipping butterscotch moonshine. Aloha and Mahalo!

To learn more about Kathy, check out her website at KathyKalmar.com.

Meanwhile, Kathy is hard at work on her next book.

www.ingramcontent.com/pod-product-compliance
Lightning Source LLC
Chambersburg PA
CBHW070510130626
46555CB00003B/1235